M000188770

SHATTERED EMOTIONS

A REDWOOD PACK NOVEL

CARRIE ANN RYAN

Shattered Emotions
A Redwood Pack Novel
By: Carrie Ann Ryan
© 2013 Carrie Ann Ryan
eBook ISBN: 978-1-62322-032-7
Paperback ISBN: 978-1-943123-28-5

This ebook is licensed for your personal enjoyment only. This ebook may not be re-sold or given away to other people. If you would like to share this book with another person, please purchase an additional copy for each person or use proper retail channels to lend a copy. If you're reading this book and did not purchase it, or it was not purchased for your use only, then please return it and purchase your own copy. Thank you for respecting the hard work of this author. To obtain permission to excerpt portions of the text, please contact the publisher .
All characters in this book are fiction and figments of the author's imagination.

SHATTERED EMOTIONS

Maddox Jamenson is the Omega of the Redwood Pack, the one burdened by emotions stronger than his own. He's spent his entire life shrouded in the secrets of his "gift" and the price he has to pay to keep it, yet the cost just escalated. He's known a mate could be in the cards for him, but he can't have what he wants. Not when the battles he has yet to fight could destroy her.

Ellie Reyes was the Central's princess, the daughter of the most hated Alpha of all time, yet not prized. No, she's spent her life as the toy of her brother's sadistic torture and has endured a pain that no one else should have to even contemplate. Though when she's rescued, the one person who could help her, her mate, turns his back on her for reasons unknown to her. As each day passes, the strength that everyone sees in her dwindles to a point that there may be no coming back from.

When the Centrals find a new way to attack, leaving Ellie's only protection a mate that she doesn't think wants her, they'll both have to overcome their fears and fight for something stronger than their pain. The war isn't over and new players are coming that will decide the outcome. Maddox and Ellie's connection will be tested even as their fragile bond is only newly forming.

ACKNOWLEDGMENTS

This was the book I had been so excited to write and so scared to write all at the same time. How do you write about the character you fell in love with the most? How do you write the story were your readers begged and pleaded more for than any other character?

Maddox and Ellie are both such reader favorites that I almost couldn't write this book.

Actually, I wrote this book four times.

What you're about to read is the final act of what happens when Maddox and Ellie get not only what they want, but what they need.

I couldn't have done this without Lia Davis, Devin, Donna, my betas, and Vickie. I couldn't have thought about this without my teams and a few readers who begged for Maddox's story.

Thank you guys for standing by me while I wrote the story that needed to be written—not the one where rainbows and unicorns are in abundance, but where Maddox and Ellie can maybe find that peace.

PROLOGUE

"She's going to die. No, she *needs* to die," Corbin muttered. He paced his dungeon room, the light from the bare bulb reflecting off the knives he'd just cleaned so he could attempt to discipline his latest 'toy'.

None of his most recent toys had been worth the trouble.

No, they were never *her. Never his sister.*

Though he'd always kept spares, so he could indulge his other urges, Ellie had been the one who could endure the pain the way he wanted. No matter how much she suffered at his hand, the fire in her eyes had never left. Yes, it had trickled to an almost dull flame, but it had never extinguished.

The fire died too quickly in these others. Frustrating. Irritating.

Maybe he just had to cut deeper, harder, and more often.

"Your sister will die, eventually," Caym, his demon lover, said as he ran a hand down his back. "You know she can't die yet. We have plans for her. If you'd step out of your room more often, you'd know we already set forth the first of those plans."

Corbin winced at the not-so-subtle reprimand in Caym's tone. Though Corbin was the Alpha of the Central Pack, it was Caym who made most of the decisions. It didn't matter much to Corbin really. No, he had all the power and play he wanted, plus a demon to take the edge off the building frustration within him—a demon with such pristine features he resembled a fallen angel.

He was so pretty, and Corbin never had the urge to scar that face.

Just like how he'd never scarred Ellie's face. No, but he'd scarred her everywhere else. Often. He'd even scarred her twin sister, but not as much. Her fire, and their cousin's fire, had died so quickly that he'd ended up playing with husks.

Not something he wanted.

Now the latter two were dead—in order to bring Caym to the human realm—and he'd lost his Ellie when the damn Redwoods had taken her with them and enveloped her in their Pack.

Those fucking Redwoods.

They were going to die; they *had* to die.

And if—no, *when*—Caym's plan worked, they'd die from

the inside out; like a rotting corpse, ripe for the plucking by the birds of death.

Yes, he'd enjoy the feast.

"Ellie will be ours," Caym whispered in his ear, sending icy shivers down his spine.

"Soon," Corbin agreed.

Soon.

1

Maddox Jamenson ran a hand through his too-long hair and looked out onto the land that had for so long called to his family and Pack. The tall trees weren't redwoods, but damn close because they seemingly touched the clouds, reaching for something that he didn't even know if he needed. He looked over his shoulder at the sound of the party he was late to, but ignored it.

They'd just have to wait a bit longer.

The cool October air tickled the back of his neck, sending shivers down his body, though those shivers didn't just come from nature. No, the power he held as the Omega of the Redwood Pack drained then filled him with more emotion than he should have been able to take.

Being the Omega was his job, his destiny. He could feel every emotion from his Pack, every need, want, desire, and heartache. It was up to him to block it all out or take it in and try to help.

One day he'd take a break from it though.

Step away from the Pack and the den, if only for a moment.

If only to breathe.

He held back a laugh. No, that wouldn't be any time soon. Not in a time of war and strife. In a time of loss and new life within his own family.

He was Maddox—he'd stay where he needed to be.

Alone, but surrounded.

He was so freaking tired, and he really didn't know why.

Thoughts of dark eyes and an even darker past flashed through his mind, and he closed his eyes.

Oh, yeah, that's why he was so tired.

"Mad?" Cailin, his baby sister, called as she came up to stand beside him.

Maddox looked down at her striking beauty, her black-blue hair and stunning Jamenson-green eyes. Even though she was only in her twenties, he knew he'd have to start fighting off potential mates soon. No way was he going to let his little sister get hurt.

"What is it, Cai?" he asked as he wrapped his arm around her shoulders. Unlike the rest of his family, he wasn't that comfortable with touching others. He'd held Bay when she'd needed him after the birth of her son, but he didn't like hugging anyone else—except his sister.

And maybe *her*...

No, never *her*...

"Why are you out here standing all alone?" she asked. She leaned into his hold, loneliness, a common emotion with her, leached off her and seeped into his chaotic hold on his own emotions.

He shrugged, not really knowing the answer. He'd always preferred to be alone, especially these days. The feelings that came from being the Omega fell on his shoulders with a heavy still silence that never went away.

Cailin scoffed, and he was pretty sure he could feel her rolling her eyes. She wasn't very subtle.

"You need to stop moping, brother mine."

"I'm not moping," he countered.

"Oh, shut up. You've been moping since you-know-who came you-know-where."

"Oh, my, however shall I figure out that code of yours?" he teased, not liking that she saw right through him.

"Well, I could say her name for you if you're that lost." This time a happier emotion drifted from her. She smiled, and he pinched her arm.

"Hey! I'm going to tell Mom!" She rubbed her arm and stuck her tongue out.

Maddox threw his head back and laughed—something he hadn't done much of lately. "Oh, my God, you're like twelve."

"Am not."

"I'm not going to argue with you."

"Why are we fighting?" she asked and smiled again.

"Because you're a pest and my baby sister."

Cailin let out a breath. "I really wish all of you would stop calling me your *baby* sister. It's not like I'm in diapers anymore. I'm a woman."

Maddox closed his eyes and groaned. "Don't remind me."

"Hey! I don't understand what your problem is. Kade and Jasper went out all the time and found women. Reed found men *and* women. Adam wasn't a monk before Anna. You've had your fair share, even if you're hiding most of it. And, North...well, I don't really want to think about what North's up to."

Maddox shook his head, trying to get the images of North doing whatever the hell he did out of his mind. In fact, he tried to keep his twin out of his mind more often than not, especially lately when the betrayal that was of his own making tasted too fresh. He'd been the one to push them together so he'd be the one to deal with it.

"You're not allowed to date," Maddox ordered, ignoring the pain that came with thinking of North.

Cailin leveled a look at him. "Um, I think I am, and I have been dating if you haven't noticed."

Rage filled him, his fists clenching as his heart raced. "What? Who? What little prick do I have to kill?"

Cailin threw up her arms and stomped away before she turned around, stomped right back, and got in his face.

"You see? This is why I don't mention it. I'm a woman. Not a girl. A woman. I've dated humans and wolves. Not that I'd let you know who. Oh, and I'm not a virgin. Just so you know."

Maddox covered his ears with his hands and hummed.

No, there was no way his baby sister was talking about...well...sex.

No. Freaking. Way.

"Sex. Maddox. Sex. Sex. Sex."

"Stop it, Cailin!"

"Oh, my God! You're such a prude!"

"And you're too young to have sex."

"Oh, shut up. It's not like I'm screwing every man I see."

Maddox closed his eyes again and prayed for patience. "I would hope not. We're already in a war with the Centrals. We don't need to kill our own Pack members."

Cailin rolled her eyes. "You need to grow up. Okay? I'm being safe—with my body and my heart. I haven't found a mate yet, and my wolf is just now starting to want one. When it happens, I don't want my brothers beating him up."

"I'm not making any promises. You have six of us, plus Josh. Not to mention what the women will do. Oh, yeah, and our folks."

"I know, hence why I'm telling you." Acceptance seeped off her, giving him another taste of emotion.

"I don't want to think about you and a man. Okay?"

"Fine, don't think about it. Just don't get in the way. Now, do we want to talk about your mating?"

"No." Hell freaking no.

"No?"

"No. Now, I'm going to go talk to Dad," he said as he brushed by her.

"Maddox Jamenson! Don't you dare tell Daddy what we talked about!"

"You know, you only call him Daddy when you're in trouble."

"Oh, shut up. Don't you dare tell him I had sex."

"You'll have to catch me first." He took off at a run, Cailin chasing behind him at full steam, which was difficult in the dress she wore for the party they were late to.

He wouldn't actually tell his dad. Some things were sacred, though if some bastard thought he could touch Maddox's baby sister, that would be another story. He'd have to do some digging on his own—after the party.

Cailin jumped on his back and wrapped her arms around his neck. "Don't, Maddox!"

He laughed, even though she was blocking his air. She released her hold, and he tossed her to the ground. She glared at him from below him, her dress pooling around her and her eyes glowing gold as her wolf rose to the surface.

"I won't, lady bug butt."

"I hate when you call me that. And you got my dress dirty."

"You're the baby, get over it. They're used to seeing you in mud. You're a tomboy, even if you try to hide it."

"I hate you, Maddox."

"Love you, too, lady bug butt."

Maddox gripped her hand and picked her up off the ground as they both walked toward the den center where Adam and Bay's belated mating ceremony was being held. They'd have to be ready to smile and act like the two of them—Maddox and Cailin—were perfectly happy being the few unmated Jamensons. Even if it was of his own choice in his case.

His baby sister had put a smile on his face, even though she gave him more worries than he needed at his age. Maybe everything would be okay.

He spotted a wisp of dark hair out of the corner of his eye and froze.

Well, hell, maybe not *that* okay.

North, his twin, walked up to him, the object of Maddox's pain on his arm. He and North looked almost identical with the same too-long sandy blond hair, same jade-green eyes, same athletic build.

North, however, was missing the jagged scar on the right side of his face.

Not that Maddox would have ever wanted his brother subjected to that.

Not for anything his twin had done in the past, present, or future.

He still loved the man, even if it hurt to look at him.

"Oh good," North said, "I'm glad we're not the only ones running late. I have a feeling Adam and Bay won't mind since they only have eyes for each other."

Maddox nodded silently and forced his gaze to North's companion.

Ellie Reyes.

His mate.

Or, at least, his could-be mate. Wolves had a few potential mates out there, some more suited than others, so that didn't mean when one found that potential they had to mate.

Maddox *couldn't* mate Ellie. Though the mating urge had reared up and rode him hard, he hadn't marked her, hadn't mated her—despite how desperately he wanted to.

She wasn't to be his.

His wolf nudged along the inside of his skin, whimpering but, as always, didn't say anything.

Ellie stood by North's side, that haunted look in her dark brown eyes reaching out to Maddox. He couldn't feel her emotions though—just as he couldn't feel North's. It could have been considered a blessing, but Maddox was never sure.

He wanted to know what made her tick, what went on in that mind of hers. He wanted to be able to help her, even if he couldn't bear to be near her.

North gave him a bland look, but Maddox could see his twin clench his jaw. Ellie stared at him as if she wanted him to say something, but he had no idea what.

"We're already late, guys. We don't want to be any later," Cailin said over the rising tension.

Maddox shook his head, trying to clear his thoughts of

the woman with dark eyes who could have been his and wasn't.

North looked between Maddox and Ellie, a shuttered look on his face, then nodded. "Agreed. I'm not in the mood to deal with the wrath of any of the Jamenson women."

Maddox blinked, tearing his gaze from Ellie. He was only torturing himself.

They made their way to the den center where the mating ceremony between Adam and Bay would take place. Though the couple had been mated for almost two years, they hadn't had the ceremony or celebrated their joining with their family and Pack yet.

Maddox couldn't really blame them for waiting, not when their meeting had been too tumultuous to begin with. Adam had almost lost Bay with his pain—Maddox hid a wince at that.

Goddess, that pain had almost been too much for him to bear—for Adam *and* Maddox. It was little wonder Maddox had tried to put a distance between him and his brother after Adam had repeatedly shaken off his help. There was only so much most Omegas could take before he broke down and sobbed uncontrollably.

Not that he did that.

No, he was stronger than that. He buried it all and worked with what he could. He could shut out the mid-level emotions, the ones that ran through the Pack daily. The high-level happiness was almost too overwhelming sometimes.

He thought back to the time Mel and Kade, his brother and Heir, had announced their pregnancy. The joy in the air had been so thick, so overwhelming, that Maddox had to set himself apart from the celebration.

Like usual.

The elation and cheer sometimes did help tone down the pain and angst within the Pack. For every person within the web who smiled, there was another who cried, and Maddox felt it all.

It was a wonder he didn't go freaking crazy.

"Maddox?"

He started at the sound of Ellie's voice.

Ellie.

Why was she talking to him?

She *never* talked to him.

They had an understanding. He wouldn't talk to her, and she wouldn't talk to him. That way they'd get over each other and their wolves would settle down, while she mated with North and made happy little pups.

It had never been spoken aloud, but damn it, it was their agreement.

Okay, fine Ellie hadn't mentioned it, but he'd live in his own denial and be fine with it.

"Yes?" he asked, his voice gruff.

"You're just standing there watching the Pack. I think it's freaking out the children."

Maddox frowned and looked at the group of pups around

them, all standing still, their eyes wide. One of the little girl's lip trembled, and Maddox cursed inwardly. It seemed that his scar and overall attitude scared everyone these days.

"Sorry, just thinking," he mumbled.

"They're about to start," Ellie whispered, then left to stand by North without another word. It was as if standing by him hurt too much to deal with.

Well, it wasn't a fucking picnic for him either.

"Uncle Maddox?" Finn, Mel and Kade's son, asked as he walked toward him.

Maddox grinned at the little boy who would one day be Alpha and had so recently been broken beyond repair—or so most had thought.

He reached down and picked his nephew up, needing the comfort himself. He didn't know why, but Finn settled him more than anyone else. If Maddox didn't know better, he'd say Finn could have been the future Omega, but no, since he was slated to be alpha, it must have been just the strength of his character that shone through.

The little boy would make a great Alpha one day.

"You ready to see Uncle Adam and Aunt Bay kiss?" Maddox asked, and Finn shrugged. At two years old, Finn didn't get the whole idea of cooties yet. It would come.

The rest of the family stood upfront surrounding Bay and Adam as Maddox made his way to stand near them, Finn still in his hold. He moved so he could stand by Mel and Kade, that way they knew their son was safe. He couldn't blame them for the worry seeping off them. After all, they'd almost lost Finn before.

Jasper and Willow stood beside them, their daughter Brie in Jasper's arms. It never failed to amuse Maddox to see the big bad Beta holding the little girl with such reverence. Across from them, Hannah stood between his brother, Reed, and their mate, Josh, each of the men holding one of their twins. Again, the sight of the big men going soft and holding their babies made Maddox think it was all worthwhile. Beside them, Cailin, North, and Ellie stood, though Ellie stood apart from them, as if she didn't want to be there.

After all, because she hadn't officially mated North—or himself, no, don't think about that—she wasn't family, but that didn't stop the Jamensons from wanting her there.

His parents stood at the top of the circle and began the ceremony. Maddox tuned out the words; he had to. The joy was so overwhelming he felt as though he was going to burst. Each of family members seemed to radiate happiness and promises of a future. Sweat rolled down his back as he fought to take it all in.

Sometimes too many good feelings were as bad as the painful ones, but he had to stick through it. He'd scream and curse at the goddess for his powers later.

His gaze met Ellie's, and he froze, all thoughts of happiness fleeing him.

He couldn't tell what she was feeling because even a bond he should have held with her through the Omega was non-existent, but he saw it in her eyes—envy...and pity.

She knew what he was dealing with.

Yet, she wanted what Bay and Adam had.

Maybe North would help with that.

Maddox couldn't do it.

The crowd started to clap, and Finn touched his cheek. He met his nephew's eyes and nodded. Yes, it was time to act like the happy brother, not the angst-filled Omega he seemed to be lately.

Maddox looked at the happy couple as they kissed, Adam picking Bay up easily, as if he hadn't lost his leg in the war with the Centrals. Bay's long red hair framed her face as the wind picked up, blowing strands around both her and Adam, bringing them even closer together.

A child's scream pierced the celebration, and Maddox tensed.

"What the hell?" Kade asked as he took Finn from Maddox's arms and handed him to Mel. "Take Finn. We're going to find out what that was."

Mel clutched Finn close but looked as if she wanted to join them. He pressed a hard kiss to his mate's lips then turned toward Maddox and the rest of his brothers.

Adam growled, a line forming between his brows. He ran a hand up and down his mate's arm as Bay frowned as well. Adam was the Enforcer, meaning he could sense danger and threats from outside forces. "I don't sense anything. It's not from outside the Pack."

Maddox met his brother's gaze, each of them knowing

what that meant. If Adam couldn't feel it, that meant it was from *inside* the Pack.

The brothers and other pack members ran in the direction of the scream. Pain, tension, worry, and anger pulsed at Maddox through the bonds, and he had to tamp them down. He couldn't focus on what was in front of him if he worried about what was within him. Another scream echoed amongst the trees, and the sense of dread that had only been a small ball before now grew, tearing at his stomach, sending shivers down his spine.

Gina, the daughter of Mel and Kade's closest friends, Larissa and Neil, ran up to them, tears running down her face, her dress torn and muddy. Her skin was as pale as a ghost, her eyes wide, haunted.

Kade picked her up and held her close. "What is it, baby?"

"Mom..." The little girl hiccupped and buried her head into Kade's neck.

Maddox kept running, reached down, and felt for the thread that connected him to Larissa and Neil. With all the emotions running through the day, he hadn't been able to deal with them all, so he'd blocked down some of them.

He stopped and closed his eyes, searching for the thread but coming up empty.

Oh, no.

No.

Maddox heard Jasper's howl of anguish when he

opened his eyes, knowing what he'd find when he stepped closer.

Larissa and Neil lay in a heap of tangled limbs and blood, their eyes vacant, their bodies cooling.

Melanie came running behind him, her scream tearing through him. The emotions of the others—terror, grief, and vengeance—slapped at him.

The scene was out of a horror novel. The scent of death lingered in the air, but that's not what scared him.

No, it was the underlying scent of another that made his body shake as his wolf clawed at his skin. It wasn't a new scent or a wrong scent. No, this one was familiar, almost comforting, and yet it was now all over the dead couple, blending with their fading ones.

It was the spicy scent of the most decadent dessert, the scent that haunted his dreams and, right now, filled him with dread.

Ellie.

Maddox looked over his shoulder as she walked toward him, the scent intensifying as her presence added another layer to the older scent trail. Her eyes were wide, unbelieving.

The others froze. Wolves that were not family growled as she came to his side.

She couldn't have done this.

The evidence was there...wasn't it?

He took her hand, and she gasped at the unfamiliar contact.

Her soft skin yielded under his, and he brought her closer, needing to protect her even though she wasn't his. His wolf needed to do this more than it needed air.

There had to be another explanation because, if there wasn't, the woman he'd hidden from, the woman who could have been his mate, had just signed her own death warrant.

2

Ellie Reyes gripped Maddox's hand as tight as she could. Yes, it was the first time he'd voluntary touched her since he'd picked her up out of the back of the Jeep when they'd first met, but, honestly, that wasn't important now.

She'd think about the calloused hands of a hard worker —one who helped his Pack and brothers, not necessarily in his job—and how they would feel against her skin. She'd think about what it all meant later.

Maybe later she could even relish his touch and imagine the scents of wolf and forest washing over her.

Later.

Right now, all she wanted to do was hide in a corner so the others would stop staring at her. Or, she could raise her chin at them all and show them they couldn't hurt her. Her wolf whimpered at the thought, not knowing if that were possible. She didn't know if she was broken or strong anymore.

She'd been hurt far more than they could ever imagine. They had *no* idea what she could endure. Oh, they'd all guessed and given her their pitying looks, but they didn't *know*.

They couldn't know.

So instead of hiding like she so desperately wanted to do, she gripped Maddox's hand harder, needing his strength, and raised her chin to the onlookers. The Jamensons looked at her with a mix of confusion and anger— though she didn't know if the anger was aimed directly at her or the situation itself.

The others though...

She swallowed hard, and Maddox squeezed her hand.

Oh, thank the goddess he's here.

No, she couldn't think it that way.

He wasn't really here, not with her. He'd made that perfectly clear when he'd walked away from her and what they could be.

A growl sounded behind her, bringing her out of the thoughts of what could have been, forcing her to stand on edge.

The others, the ones who hadn't readily accepted her because of the blood in her veins, had already condemned her. She'd always known she'd been living on borrowed time, but she hadn't thought it would end like this.

She was a wolf for hell's sake. She couldn't just back

down and show her belly in weakness. The others would kill her in an instant if they thought they could. Only the good graces of the Jamensons...and her connection to Maddox kept her alive. She knew that and wouldn't have broken that trust no matter what.

Her scent wrapped around two dead bodies—two bodies of people Kade and Mel, the Heir mated pair, cared about, and that didn't help matters.

Ellie hadn't killed them, but someone had wanted to make sure it looked like she had.

Mel, shaking with sobs, had lain her body on top of Larissa's. Grief slid through Ellie like an old friend. She knew that feeling—had almost drowned in that feeling. Yet, it wasn't grief over what she was about to lose—what she'd already lost.

She had nothing left of herself. Her brother, Corbin, had taken almost everything from her, and Maddox's rejection had stripped the last of it.

She's been an empty shell for so long it barely seemed important to her anymore that the evidence condemned her. What mattered was that two people were dead, a lovely witch who took no attitude from anyone and a wolf who cared about everyone in his path.

Two parents who'd left two little children in this world as they left to commune with the goddess.

They'd been taken from this world, and their bodies now lay prone in a grotesque fashion.

And the others blamed her.

For a moment, just a moment, she thought about lying and saying she'd done it. If she did, maybe the pain would go away, that never-ending ache from a wound that would never heal. The scars on her back and legs proved that some things could heal, but didn't ensure recovery. The scars on her heart still bled with each breathe, each day that she tried to act normal.

Maybe it wasn't worth it anymore.

Her wolf dug its claws into her from the inside, and she squeezed Maddox's hand for strength, for that anchor.

Her wolf, despite being beaten beyond hope, didn't want to die today.

Nor did Ellie.

Kade, the Heir to the Redwood Pack, the one who would one day take his father's place as Alpha, could feel the souls of the Pack through this connection. He had sworn his life to his Pack's protection, and he now knelt and picked up his mate, cradling her to his chest.

The act was so gentle, yet so heartbreaking, that Ellie wanted to scream. It wasn't fair that Mel had to feel this, just as it wasn't fair that Ellie would never have that mate to hold her and tell her it was all right.

Because it would never be all right.

People were dying all around her, and she couldn't do anything to stop it.

She was just the Central's princess—the only one left.

Kade walked past them all, Mel sobbing into his shoulder. They didn't have to act strong in front of the others right now, not when their grief was so tactile, so new. The others knew that there would be vengeance, of that everyone was sure.

"We're just going to let this one live?" one of the wolves, Patrick if she remembered correctly, asked, a growl escaping his lips.

Jasper, the Beta of the Pack, the one who took care of their needs even when they didn't know they had them, growled back, his eyes glowing gold.

These Jamensons were so different from the hierarchy of the Centrals. Where the Centrals ruled by fear and torture, the Jamensons ruled with power and strength, but not threats—not unless needed.

Patrick snarled but bared his neck in submission. Patrick might have been a hothead, but there was no comparison to the type of power the Jamensons held. Everyone knew who held the powers of the alpha, the hierarchy of strength, and this Patrick was nowhere close.

"Calm yourself, Patrick," Jasper ordered. "We don't know what happened yet."

"You can smell her on them," another wolf, Donald, said, his voice not as firm as Patrick's but his words equally as condemning.

Maddox pulled her behind him, his hand still firmly tangled with hers. Her heart leapt in her throat at the action, but she couldn't let him get hurt for her.

No, that would hurt more than her own heartbreak.

She tried to move around him, and he pulled her back, a

soft growl escaping his lips. Apparently, his wolf was riding him hard, and she didn't want to force him to break his concentration or his control, not when there might be a fight for dominance soon.

Later she'd tell him not to bother protecting her, not when she wasn't his responsibility.

She wasn't his mate by bond.

"You need to back off, Donald," Maddox said, his voice low but still deadly, as if he'd growled with all his power.

"Oh, really?" Patrick asked, contempt in his gaze. "You're going to defend this Central bitch even though you wouldn't mate her? She's not good enough for you, but she's special enough for you to keep around after she kills our people?"

Before Ellie could blink, Maddox had the other man on the ground, his hand wrapped around Patrick's throat.

"Did you just call a member of our Pack a bitch?" Maddox growled low, dangerous.

Ellie's wolf rose to the surface, the need to protect her mate—even a mate who didn't want her—all but bringing her to her knees.

North came to her side, blocking her from any sneak attack, and she wanted to curse. As much as she loved North as the man who'd taken care of her when she'd needed it, she wasn't his mate—despite what others seemed to believe. She didn't want him by her side when her wolf so badly wanted to kneel by Maddox, fighting for herself and rejoicing in the fact he was doing the same.

North in her path and the fact that she had no idea *why*

Maddox was acting the way he was stopped her. The last thing she needed was to stand in the way and cause harm to someone she cared about.

Patrick tried to answer, but Maddox didn't let him. He merely pressed down on the other wolf's neck harder.

"No, don't answer, I don't want to hear it. If I hear you calling any of our women that name again, I'll make you regret everything you've ever done. Do you understand me? And, remember, I don't need to physically touch you to hurt you. I'm the fucking Omega. All I need to do is give you a fraction of what I feel, and you'll be writhing on the floor."

His brothers turned and narrowed their eyes at his threat, but didn't say anything.

A slight pain slid through her like a small burn. He'd only protected her because he'd protect any woman in his Pack. It wasn't because she was special. It was because he was the Omega, and it was his duty to care for the ones in his hold.

It wasn't because she was his Ellie.

She'd never be *his* Ellie.

"Maddox," Adam whispered behind his brother.

"What?" Maddox asked, disgust in his tone. "You know that's my strength. The only reason I don't do it is because I don't think people deserve the pain, anguish, and death I feel on a daily basis. I'll gladly share it with you, though, dear Patrick."

Ellie stood still, her knees locked. This wasn't the

Maddox she was used to. He didn't growl at others; he didn't yell or threaten.

Yet she didn't fault him for his words. She didn't envy his burden, though she would gladly take it off his shoulders... or at least share it if they could have been mates. As a mate of any other position in the pack, they would share power. It had to be the same for an Omega hopefully.

It wasn't easy being the Omega—an understatement if there ever was one.

Maddox growled once more then stood up, leaving Patrick on the ground, his chin raised to bare his throat in submission.

"We've brought Ellie into our Pack because she's innocent," Jasper said, his voice calm, soothing where anger would have worked just as well.

"How do we know this?" Patrick spat, and Ellie wanted to slap the bastard. The wolf was walking a fine line, even though he had a right to speak his mind.

Maddox stalked toward him again and leaned down. "Are you questioning your Alpha?"

"Son, he has a right to question, as I'm not a sadistic ruler, but Patrick, watch your strengths," Edward warned as he walked toward them. "We will discuss this later. Right now, though, you will show the proper respect and take care of our Pack mates behind you who have lost their lives. Their bodies are cold in shadow, yet you all stand here and accuse one another. I'm ashamed of you all."

Ellie lowered her eyes and bared her throat. Her eyes itched as tears threatened. She hadn't forgotten Neil and Larissa, but she'd let her own worries overshadow thoughts of them.

She didn't deserve to call these wolves her Pack.

She didn't deserve anything but their ridicule and distrust.

After all, she was the Central's princess, the sister and daughter of the enemy. She was the one who was accused of killing their Pack mates.

She was the one who deserved it all.

No matter that, there wasn't much left of her to fight back.

Not after the torture, the beatings, the loss of her twin, her cousin, and so much more.

Jasper nodded, everyone following suit. Edward faced her, and she ducked her head.

This was it.

She'd either be killed, forced to face the circle, or outcast altogether with no protection from Corbin or the demon by his side, Caym.

"Go to my home, Maddox. Take Ellie with you," her Alpha said, his voice so soft it broke her heart. "We'll talk there."

Maddox took her hand again, and she closed her eyes, needing to feel him just for a moment before everything was taken away.

She hated this version of herself. She used to be strong,

self-reliant. Now, she was just a broken wolf who didn't want to be here anymore.

When she'd lost all hope, she'd discovered she didn't really know who she was anymore.

If she didn't know that now, if she'd lost everything she ever was, how strong could she have been before?

"Come on," North said by her side. "We'll talk about it all when we get there."

Maddox glared at his twin, and Ellie wanted to scream. She hadn't meant to get in between the brothers. Maddox might have misconstrued her relationship with North, but she didn't think he'd believe her, no matter what she said. This wasn't the time to get into it anyway.

She followed Maddox to Edward and Pat's house, North following them. Jasper and Adam had stayed behind to deal with Larissa's and Neil's bodies. She bit her lip to control the sob that threatened to escape. She hadn't known them well, but they'd been nice to her when they hadn't had to. They'd welcomed her to the Pack because they were nice people and friends with the Jamensons.

Now, they were gone, leaving behind two children who would never again hear their voices, see their smiles, or feel their touch.

It wasn't fair.

Nothing was in life—a lesson Ellie had learned long ago. She just wished Gina and Mark hadn't had to learn it so soon.

They walked into the house, and Ellie clenched her fists

at the sight before her. Mel held Gina and Mark in her arms while Kade wrapped his arm around her shoulders. Gina had found her parents' bodies, so there was no hiding the deaths—not that they would anyway.

At their entrance, Mel looked up, her eyes bloodshot, but her mouth in a thin line.

"Did they find anything?" Mel asked, her voice surprisingly strong.

Maddox pulled Ellie into the room as North answered. "No, just what you saw. We will find out though." He knelt before the children as they sniffed at him, their little bodies shaking with their cries. He did a quick check up as everyone else spoke to be sure they were okay.

"Take a seat. I know Dad said he'd be here soon," Kade said, looking directly at her.

She had no idea what was about to happen, but she'd take the time she could to compose herself. She didn't like being this fragile, poor excuse for a wolf.

There had to be something she could do.

Maddox sat down on the other couch and pulled her to his side while North sat on her other. Kade looked at them, his brow raised.

Great, just what she needed, a weird dominance battle between twins while she was confused beyond measure. She didn't have time to worry about who wanted to mate her and what others thought about it.

The kids grieving for their parents were more important than her.

The door opened, and the rest of the family filed in. Reed and his two mates, Hannah and Josh, walked in, each man carrying one of their two-month-old twins. They were the triad of the Redwood Pack and had been the ones to rescue her when she'd done her best to save Josh from the demon.

She owed them her life, even if others thought it hadn't been worth it.

Behind them, Cailin, the only daughter of the Alpha, walked in with Finn, Kade and Mel's son on her hip. Finn wiggled out of his aunt's hold and ran to his parents. Kade gathered him up in his arms, and Finn held his mother who held his friends, grief pouring out of the little boy who'd been through so much in his short life.

Cailin glared at Ellie, a usual occurrence, her piercing green eyes examining and finding Ellie wanting. Ellie had never broken through the barrier with the Jamenson sister, no matter how hard she'd tried. She knew Cailin was the closest to Maddox, even closer than North from what she'd seen, and Ellie must have been not worth the dirt she stepped on.

That was fine with her. Despite how Maddox was acting now, he didn't want her anyway.

Cailin sat on the floor in front of the loveseat where Josh, Hannah, and Reed had sat. Tears ran down her face, despite the glare she gave to Ellie.

Adam came in walking with a slight limp, his mate, Bay, by his side and his son, Micah, in his arms. He'd lost his leg when Caym had ripped it from his body, and Ellie still had nightmares of how much pain the man would have been through. It was a testament to the agony Adam was in that he'd even show the limp in front of his family—and her— but she knew if anyone outside of family had been there he would have fought through the pain.

Jasper and Willow followed, Willow holding their daughter, Brie. Where most families might have hidden their children from the pain of loss, the Redwood pack members were more than humans; they were also wolves. The children needed to know what was going on, even if they were only babies. They were all connected within the Pack, and no matter what, they would stand together.

That idea was foreign to someone who'd grown up with the Centrals.

Ellie didn't know quite how she felt about that.

Maddox squeezed her hand, and she looked down at their clasped fingers and blinked. She'd almost forgotten he'd still held her; that he hadn't shied away from her when he could have.

No one spoke. It was as if, once they did, the damn would burst. Besides, nothing would get done without the Alpha. They all sat in their dresses and suits, reminding her they'd been at a mating ceremony before this.

It seemed like ages ago she'd felt jealous watching Adam and Bay kiss and share their love with the Pack. They'd deserved finally celebrating their mating, and now, the day was marred with tragedy.

Ellie could feel the tension in the air, practically taste it. She could also see the tension in Maddox's shoulders, and the urge to comfort him overwhelmed him. She knew he hated being in crowds—even with his family. He felt every emotion in the room, and right now, it had to be agonizing with the grief, anger, confusion, and so many more warring around them.

She rubbed her thumb along his wrist, and he froze. Damn, she shouldn't have done that. They weren't mated, and he didn't want her. She didn't need to comfort him. Just as she was about to stop, his shoulders eased, and he let out a slight sigh.

Thank the goddess.

Ellie continued the small circles, knowing that she was avoiding the situation in front of her, but at least helping Maddox in a small way.

Edward and Pat walked in, and she stiffened.

Pat walked toward Gina and Mark and knelt, cupping both of their cheeks. "I'm so sorry, little ones," she whispered, her voice soft but strong with the power of the Alpha.

Mark held out his arms, and Pat picked him up, holding him to her chest while she whispered soothing words.

Edward shook his head, sadness and anger marring his face. "We have a problem, and I see only one way to resolve it."

Ellie swallowed hard, and Maddox gripped her hand tighter, anchoring her.

"We have a few problems, Edward," Pat said as she

rocked Mark, who was only five and too young to understand it all. Gina was eight and knew all too well her world had been shattered.

"That we do, my love, that we do. First, How are we going to help them?" he asked as Gina and Mark looked toward them. "Normally, I would wait until you two weren't here to talk about this, but you deserve a say, little ones."

Gina nodded, tears running down her cheeks.

"You don't have to worry about that," Kade said, his voice stern. "We'll take care of them."

Cailin gasped, and Ellie held back one of her own.

"Kade—" Jasper started, and Kade shook his head.

"I know it's going to be an issue, but I'm not letting other people's feelings get in the way of it. Gina and Mark will stay with us, and we will care for them as our own. Larissa and Neil would have wanted that."

Ellie swallowed as she thought of the implications of that. Kade was the Heir to the Pack, meaning he would one day be Alpha and one day Finn would be Heir. The rest of their children would hold the other key positions like the Beta, and most likely the Enforcer, Omega, and Healer once they were old enough to take them from those who currently held power.

By taking in two children who were not of their blood, they were giving them a higher place in the hierarchy without the inherited power or real positions. The countless issues with that for the other wolves in the Pack, as well as within their own family, would need to be dealt with.

Honestly, though, she thought Kade and Mel could handle it. The importance of taking care of those children would far outweigh the issues of hurt feelings and confusion.

Edward finally nodded and let out a breath. "I'd assumed you'd do that. I know Gina and Mark won't hold your power or take on any of the duties, but they will be family. Yes, it might be an issue for how others see it, but within our family we'll make it work." He looked toward the children. "You will always have your parents in your hearts and memories—in *our* hearts and memories—but you can be Jamensons now, and know we will always be by your side."

Mark nodded, too young to really understand what was happening, but Gina looked at them all before finally nodded, knowing there wasn't another real option because Neil and Larissa had no other family within the Pack. With the state of war they were currently in, they couldn't be left alone. Not that any of them in this room would allow that anyway.

"Hannah, Willow, and Bay, can you take the children out to the other room for a minute? Cailin, go with them."

The women looked surprised for a moment, but they began to file out with the children. Ellie didn't know why they had to go, other than the fact that they needed all the arms they could get to corral all the children. Soon, all the young were out of the room, and tension again filled the air.

Edward turned to Ellie then and frowned. She lowered her gaze but faced him.

This was it.

This was her fate.

"We know you didn't do this, Ellie," Edward said, and she finally broke, letting out a sob.

"Why...why would someone do this?" she said, finally breaking her silence.

Edward shook his head. "I don't know, but that is something we all need to find out. However, we can't do that with you here, Ellie."

Ellie's head rose, and she gaped. Was he kicking her out of the Pack?

"You're still Pack, Ellie. I didn't bring you in just to kick you out, but we need to do something about what happened. Clearly, we have someone within the Pack who is a traitor. Someone who used your scent to cover their own. They wanted us to blame you and kill you or kick you out. This smells of the Centrals. We know they didn't want you to live after you left them."

She nodded, remembering the sting of the whip at her back—one of Corbin's delights.

She shuddered, and Maddox moved so he could wrap his arm around her shoulders. She sank into his side, not caring she'd have to take it all back later.

"You're going to have to leave the den, Ellie."

She blinked and nodded, knowing her time was up. "I

know. Thank you for letting me stay here for as long as I have."

Maddox and North both growled beside her, but Edward held up his hand, his power washing over them all.

"You're not leaving the Pack, Ellie. We need to smoke out the traitor. To do that, I want to make him or her *think* we're forcing you to leave the den for a bit. You will be leaving the den, but not the Pack. We want them to think we've turned our backs on you...at least some of us."

She shook her head, confused. "I don't understand."

"You're going to leave for a bit while we flush out the traitor. Then we'll bring you back stronger than ever. The distrust in this Pack is too high for me to take at the moment, and I'm going to have to squash it. I'm the Alpha, and my word is law, but sometimes it takes more than words."

"We're not letting her leave the den without protection," Maddox growled, and she took in his warmth, greedy for anything she could get.

Great, she wanted a man she couldn't have, and she hated herself for it, but she'd put up that boundary later and learn to live without him—just like she'd always had to.

"No, we're not going to do that," Edward said, his voice stern. "You're going to go with her, son. We'll make them think that you guys are leaving as well—choosing her over us. That will make the traitor and the Centrals think we're breaking down from the inside. I'll leave it to you to come up with a plan. North, as well. I don't care what you have to do, but while we figure out the problem within our den walls, you three will figure out the problems that lay between you. Understand?"

Ellie blinked as Maddox froze, North doing the same on her other side.

Well, hell, if the Alpha's word was law that meant they had to face their own issues.

Finally, she'd find out why Maddox didn't want her.

Even if she was afraid of the answer.

3

Maddox stuffed the last of his clothes in his bag and zipped it shut. With the amount of food, supplies, and other crap in it, if he hadn't been a wolf, he wouldn't have been able to lift the thing. He looked around his house and sighed. He knew he'd be back—soon if his family had any say about it—but he didn't know what he'd come back to or who he'd be when he did so.

His father had flat-out told him he needed to get his head out of his ass and deal with Ellie and North. Meaning he'd have to get over himself and Ellie while watching her finally mate his brother. It was the only option since he couldn't mate her himself. There was no way he'd subject her to the powers and pain he had. He'd heard stories of how that happened between an Omega and mate.

He cared for her too much for that.

Yes, he'd own up to that, but that was it.

He'd barely been able to breathe while in the room with his family, their emotions choking him. Then Ellie had rubbed her thumb along his wrist, settling him. He hadn't even thought it possible to quiet the emotions, the feelings, but she'd helped him that little bit.

At what cost, he didn't know.

That was the unknown, the fear that lodged in his throat at the thought of mating her.

He shouldn't have held her hand or pulled her into his arms when she needed him. She had North for that and everything it entailed, but he'd let himself give into what he wanted, not what needed to be done.

He wouldn't let it happen again.

He *couldn't* let it happen again.

With one last look at his home, he closed the door and headed to where Ellie stayed. He didn't think of it as her home, as she didn't call it that. It was as if she'd known all along her stay might be only temporary.

When they got back, he'd have North fix that. He couldn't bear to think of her not feeling welcome after all this time.

The three of them had already said their goodbyes to his family, and he'd blocked off the sorrow and worry seeping from them as they wished the three good luck. It had been too much for him to deal with, so he was glad it was over, at least for a little while.

God, he hated to say that about his family. As much as he loved them, he still needed his space to breathe. He wasn't sure they understood that. Oh, they said all the right things, but sometimes he felt as though they wanted to pull him closer to comfort him when all he needed was the space to deal with all the emotions warring within him.

The three of them would be on foot instead of driving to make sure the Pack thought they were leaving behind anything that had to do with their pasts. Even though he was the Omega and was *needed* there, he could take a break and leave for a bit—not that he'd ever done it.

He froze where he was and blinked. This was the first time he'd be away from the Pack and would only get a whisper of their emotions. He'd be with North and Ellie— the two whose every hurt and every joy he couldn't feel— meaning it would almost be quiet for him.

It might be selfish of him, but he couldn't wait, even with the danger involved.

He needed to breathe again, something he hadn't done in too long.

His family would find the traitor and keep the Pack safe. He'd be with the two who meant the most to him and could thereby hurt him the most, but he'd keep them safe.

Something he'd been doing his whole life.

Ellie sat on her small porch, a backpack as full as his own by her side. Jeans encased her long, athletic legs, and she wore a jacket over a sweater. He knew she probably had more layers underneath, same as he. They had no idea how long they'd be gone, but he hoped it wouldn't be that long.

At the sound of his footsteps, her head rose, and her

gaze met his. He stopped where he was and looked into those dark brown eyes, hating himself for being weak. Her long black hair framed her face and trailed behind her shoulders, down her back. He'd dreamed of wrapping his hand around it as he mated her for the first time and the many times after.

Maddox closed his eyes, breaking their contact, and cursed himself.

Though his father had wanted them to deal with their issues, that didn't give him the right to think about her naked, her full breasts molded against his chest as he pumped in and out of her, feeling the walls of her pussy clenching around his cock as she moaned his name when she climaxed. He could imagine himself sinking his teeth into the fleshy part of her neck where it met her shoulder, marking her as his for all the world to see.

Shit.

"Maddox?"

Ellie's voice broke him from his thoughts, and he held back a groan. Great, they were about to embark on a journey in which he'd be their only protection against the Centrals with a woman who was his brother's soon-to-be-mate, and here he was, imagining her naked and beneath him, pleading his name while he marked her for life.

He should have been better than this, but he really wasn't.

"Do you have everything?" he asked, his voice gruffer than he'd intended.

She nodded and picked up her bag. "I don't have much to begin with, but I have enough."

"Good, we better get going."

Out of the corner of his eye, he saw North come up to them, his bag over one shoulder, a frown on his face, his unscarred face.

Sometimes it was odd to look into his brother's face. He'd once possessed a mirror image of North's. Now, he saw what he could have been, but he had to deal with what was.

"I'm ready, as well," North said as he came to Ellie's side, too close for Maddox's comfort, but then again, he had no choice in the matter.

Like his father wanted, soon they'd be able to come clean with what North and Ellie could be, and Maddox would finally be free.

Alone, but free.

Maddox nodded and started down the path toward the forest that would, eventually, lead them through the den wards, and they'd leave the comfort and safety of all he'd ever known. He didn't speak as Ellie and North followed him. He didn't even look behind him to see if they were holding on to each other or standing too close.

Frankly, he didn't even know if he could take it, though it was his own fault to begin with.

They passed through the wards with ease, the magic sliding over him like a warm blanket. If he'd been of another Pack, they would have stopped him with a painful arch unless he'd been welcomed in by a Pack member. If he'd been human, then the wards would have magically forced him to look the other way.

It was how the wolves had remained secret for so long. They'd settled in the west long before the white human had. The Redwoods had hidden themselves among the trees within the den so only a select few could find them. As the Europeans settled out west, the Redwoods gradually came out of hiding, though never revealing their true nature. When they weren't in war, they melded with the humans, working, living, and breathing among them. With the war with the Centrals in full force, their Pack was in seclusion, remaining as safe as they could be under the wards.

However, the events of that morning had just shined a light on the fact that they weren't safe—they wouldn't be until Caym and Corbin were defeated. Unless the Redwoods found a way to use dark magic and fight against the demon, Maddox wasn't sure how they would win.

They would though.

They had to.

"Mad?" North asked, drawing him out of his thoughts.

Maddox stopped behind a large tree, keeping his senses open so he could scout any danger. They weren't inside the Pack walls anymore, meaning the Centrals could attack at any moment.

"Yeah?"

"Do we have a plan?" his brother asked as he walked to Maddox's side, Ellie on his heels.

Maddox snorted. "Really? You're just now asking me that?"

North shrugged and scratched the back of his neck. "I figured you did since you usually do. Plus Dad kind of blindsided me with all of this, so I wasn't thinking."

"Clearly," Maddox mumbled, and North rolled his eyes.

For a moment, it was as if they were pups again, friends, brothers, and two halves of a whole. Then Maddox's gaze shifted to Ellie, and he let that thought float away on the wind like it should.

It wasn't the same, and it never would be, but Maddox would be damned if he lived his life in a daze because of it.

"I was planning on heading east toward the cabin we used to hang out at as kids when mom and dad took us on trips then reevaluate." Before the Centrals had gone crazy, the Redwoods had been able to live outside the den and visit others often. "We don't have to be anywhere other than *not* at the den. We have our phones in case of an emergency and we have to go back *and* so we know when we can go back."

Ellie closed her eyes as her shoulders sank. "I'm sorry you two had to come out here and deal with this."

Maddox fought the urge to pull her into his arms and tell her everything would be okay. All he wanted to do was inhale her scent and let it settle him, but North beat him to the punch, wrapping his arm around her shoulders and squeezing.

"Hey, this isn't your fault," North said. "It's your brother's and a traitor's."

Ellie shook her head. "If it was just that, then I wouldn't be out here, and you both know that."

Maddox growled softly. "Just because there are ignorant people out there doesn't mean you have to feel bad about yourself. You didn't do anything wrong, and those closest to you know that." He inwardly winced at his choice of words, considering all he wanted to do was be as close to her as possible, yet he *needed* the distance.

Ellie groaned. "I hate that it's putting pressure on your family though. The Pack is questioning the Alpha, and I don't think you guys have done that before."

North snorted. "They can question all they want, but they will obey. Our father will listen to their concerns but will do what's best for the Pack, and that means welcoming you in."

"That's not how I'm used to Packs running," Ellie said, that hint of darkness Maddox hated seeping in her words.

Maddox wanted to find Corbin and kill him—slowly. He didn't know exactly what the bastard had done to Ellie, but he knew it had been beyond horrific. He'd seen the scars on her back and legs when they went on hunts, and he knew the worst scars were probably not the ones seen.

"The Redwoods are your Pack now, so we'll show you how a pack *should* be run," North said, and he ran a hand down her arm.

Maddox's gaze followed its trail, and he bit back a growl.

Ellie wasn't his by his own choice. He shouldn't feel jealous. He should feel at peace that his twin had found his mate and that the one woman whom Maddox wanted to be happy would be happy.

Yet, no matter how hard he tried, he couldn't find that peace.

North cleared his throat and released Ellie. Maddox did his best not to be relieved and failed. "Let's get going. It's going to take at least a day's hike to get there, and we have to keep vigilant."

Maddox nodded and started to move, but Ellie put her hand on his arm, all but stopping him.

Hell, she was so soft, so small.

So not his.

"Yes?" he asked, his voice a growl.

"Why are you acting like this?" she asked, a bit of temper in her voice.

He almost smiled at that. She was never angry, not really. She always kept her emotions hidden, as if that was how she'd been trained to act—and probably had been.

"Acting like what?"

"Acting gruff and jealous. I don't understand, Maddox."

His name on her tongue made him want to groan. Damn, he needed to get off this dangerous path and send her to North's open arms. His brother would know what to do.

Wait...jealous? She couldn't tell what he was thinking. No one could ever do that, not even North most days.

"What are you talking about?"

Ellie growled then threw her arms above her head. "You're acting like you feel something for me when I know that's not the case. Edward said we needed to deal with this, so why not say it now? You know we're mates, or at least we could be. You've done nothing about it, Mad. You've all but told me I'm nothing to you and you don't feel the mating urge like I do. You've done all you could to stay away from me, and when you're near me, you growl or chase me to tell me what I'm doing wrong like you did at the triad's mating ceremony."

He remembered stalking after her at the ceremony, but it hadn't been to yell, but to protect. At least that's what he'd thought.

"I didn't yell at you then," he said lamely.

"Really? Because I think you did."

"No, I was following you because of those guys who were taunting you."

Her eyes lowered, and she swallowed. "They weren't saying anything I'm not used to."

Maddox resisted the urge to cup her chin and feel her soft skin. "You shouldn't have to be used to it."

She backed up a step and shook her head. "No, it doesn't matter. You can't act like a big protector if you're rejecting our mating. It's not fair to me. I'm doing all I can to be normal and act like I deserve something, and you're not helping."

He felt as if she'd slapped him. He'd never meant to

make her feel like that. No, he'd done all he could to ensure she'd be safe without him, safe from his powers and the others.

"Ellie, we can't be mates."

She froze for a moment, the pain so clear on her face he didn't need to feel her emotions to know he'd hurt her.

"Fine, but when we're not in the middle of the forest with the world crashing down around us, you will tell me why. I at least deserve that."

She turned on her heel and stalked toward North, who hadn't moved as far as Maddox thought. His twin glared at him in disappointment, and his expression could have killed lesser wolves.

Maddox took a deep breath before taking a step. He'd hurt her, something he hadn't wanted to do, but it had to be done.

He couldn't be with her and not inflict her with constant pain. She deserved more than him, and North would provide that.

They'd just have to live with that.

4

The wind whipped through the trees and sent a shiver down Ellie's spine. At least she thought it came from the wind, though it could have come from the tension in their little group. Between the brothers not looking at one another, her own emotions tangling with Maddox's, and the whole Centrals-could-kill-them-at-any-moment thing, Ellie was about at her wit's end.

She couldn't believe she'd finally stood up for herself. Yes, she'd always tried with Corbin and had succeeded for years, but over time, he'd beaten that out of her. She'd always tried to be the strong one for her twin and cousin, but she hadn't been strong enough.

Pain flared, clawing at her belly, and she took a deep breath through her nose, letting Maddox's scent wash over her, soothing her in the process. He might not be her mate according to him—something that she was going to get to the bottom of—but her wolf needed him.

She needed him.

Ellie cursed at the thought because she needed to get away from that need, or at least try to erase it. She needed to find that strength that she'd once had. Sure, she'd saved Josh and showed Reed and Hannah the way out of the bunker where her brother had locked Josh, but it had been nothing. She could have done more...so much more.

She *should* have done more.

Instead, she'd had to sit back and watch her father and brother sacrifice her twin and cousin to bring Caym into the world.

What kind of monster did that make her if she were the one left standing?

It should have been her on that plank of wood, dying at the hands of her own brother or the demon who had come to destroy them all. Instead, it had been the two women who'd already broken long before.

At least they weren't in pain anymore.

Her wolf nudged at her, and she started, remembering where she was. This was not the time to woolgather and have herself a pity party. No, she needed to follow these two men who meant to world to her—despite how much she didn't want that to be the case. They were giving up their homes, albeit for a little while, and endangering their lives to protect her.

They were also leaving their Pack in jeopardy to do so.

Generally, Maddox was needed in the den often to handle the fragile balance between peace and strife within the Pack, but he was allowed to leave when necessary. Knowing him as she did—even from afar—she knew he didn't leave often. They were his flock, his duty, and he wasn't going to leave them for long.

Hannah, as the Healer of the Pack, could take care of their needs and deal with any injures when North wasn't there. Cailin too had trained a bit so she could help her brother. The Jamenson sister seemed to be the jack-of-all-trades and was still trying to find her footing. The girl was only in her twenties though so, really, she had all the time in the world.

Well, of course, they'd have to beat the Centrals first to ensure that, but seeing what she'd seen of the Jamensons, Ellie thought they might actually have a chance. She'd seen, firsthand, the depravity of the Pack she'd grown up with and knew what they were capable of. She only hoped the Redwoods were ready.

"What's going through that head of yours, Ellie?" North asked as he pulled back to walk beside her. She saw the light stiffening in Maddox's shoulders before he loosened them, not even turning back to see what was happening.

Oh, they would be having that talk all right. There was no way she could live with herself not knowing why he didn't want her. Sure, it would probably break her more than anything Corbin had done, but she deserved to know the truth.

She needed to know why she wasn't good enough for Maddox Jamenson.

"Ellie?"

North's voice brought her out of her thoughts again, and she cursed. "Sorry, I'm just thinking about things that I shouldn't be, considering I need to keep on my toes."

North stopped and gave her an odd look. "You know you can always tell me anything, right?"

Ellie gave a sad smile. He'd always said that, and she believed him. Goddess, she wanted to be able to fall to her knees and weep in his arms, telling him everything that had happened so she could finally find a way to heal...but he wasn't Maddox.

"I know," she whispered, her voice low. She'd already used up any backbone she had when she yelled at Maddox.

She'd do better at that next time.

North let out a long sigh. "But, you're not going to, are you?"

She looked into those green eyes that were so much like the rest of his family's and shook her head. "I'm sorry, North."

North shrugged but didn't touch her, thankfully. She didn't like it when people touched her—other than Maddox. Yes, North occasionally did to lead her to places, but that was about as far as she could go.

Her wolf was damaged and wanted her mate.

Something Ellie could agree with.

"You two done talking?" Maddox asked, something almost painful in his tone.

Ellie turned to look at him, an odd look on her face. North wasn't her mate, didn't Maddox know that?

"Sorry to hold you up," North bit off.

Goddess, she hated being the person standing between them. As soon as they were in a safer place, they'd have to do what their Alpha had said and get it all out on the table. She wouldn't be responsible for breaking the bond between twins.

She'd already lost her own twin to evil. She wasn't about to be responsible for the brothers' loss, as well.

North gave her one last look then headed off through the trees, leaving Ellie to follow them. Their enemies could come at them from any side, so it was no use putting her in the middle to protect the "little woman". She might have been damaged and, frankly, scared to death of certain things, but she would fight if she had to—if only to protect the men so they wouldn't have to protect her.

The scent of rain lingered in the air, the pressure changing ever so slightly, indicating that a storm was on its way. She hoped they would be near shelter when that happened, though it would have been nice to know exactly where they were going. Maddox said he knew; therefore, she'd just have to trust him. While she trusted him with her life, she couldn't trust him with her heart. He'd already stomped on it, and there was no reason to let it happen again.

"Other than eternal happiness," her wolf whispered.

Ellie rolled her eyes. Oh, yes, that.

She followed the brothers without speaking for another hour until they stopped for a water break. She knew they probably could have gone on longer, but they were stopping for her.

Her nose wrinkled at that. She wasn't the strongest wolf, not by far, but she'd been working on gaining her strength so she could fight with the best of them. That is, if she ever got over that mind-numbing fear. It's not that she didn't want to fight—it was just that every time she thought about fighting back she remembered how *he* liked her to fight back.

North had been helping her on that, training her at his house so she could learn to fight with speed and agility, rather than the blind fear she'd used before.

Corbin had always liked when she fought him...

A shiver ran down her back at the memory, and she closed her eyes, willing it to go away.

"Ellie?" North asked. "Ready to go?"

She nodded, not meeting the eyes of either man, though she could feel their gazes on her. Maybe Maddox was right and she didn't deserve him. Not that he'd said that to her, but it had to be the reason...right? They had no idea what she'd been through, but they *had* to see it marked on her skin. Past the scars they could see were the ones that had seeped into her pores, the dirt and filth of years when she was nothing more than a doll to burn and toy with.

Maddox came to her side, and she stiffened, afraid that he'd see what she felt, what was etched into her skin. She felt a tug as he did something with her bag, and she frowned.

"What are you doing?"

"Making sure your pack is on right and not too heavy," he mumbled, and her traitorous body warmed.

No, he wasn't thinking about her safety and care like she wanted. He was probably just caring for her as he would for any other member of the Pack.

"I'm fine," she snapped, angry at him, at herself, and the situation. "I'm not as weak as you think I am."

Maddox's eyes widened, and she cursed inwardly. Why was it she could only find her backbone when she was around this man? She never yelled back or fought for herself unless it was around him. Yet, it never seemed to get her far.

She was still alone.

Hell, she didn't want to be one of those women who thought a man would fix it all, and frankly, she wasn't, but it would be nice to have someone to lean on when times got rough...someone other than North, whom she didn't have feelings for.

"I never thought you were weak, Ellie," Maddox whispered, his voice a caress when she couldn't handle it. "Far from it."

With that, he left her to stand on her own, not even looking back.

North gave her a sad look then started off behind his brother, leaving Ellie again to trail behind.

A branch cracked to their side, and Ellie froze, her wolf rising to the surface. She let her senses widen, tasting the air and the energy around them. She might not have any special powers like the others in the Pack, but she could still hear and see things better than a human.

Maddox moved back slowly to her side, while North flanked her other side. As much as she wanted to growl at them for trying to protect her, she knew it wouldn't do any good. Not only were they better fighters than her, but their wolves *needed* to protect her. It wasn't an instinct the human in them could easily overrun. Yes, they might have let her walk by herself for a bit, but that was before the danger had shown itself.

Goosebumps ran up her arms, and she clenched her teeth. Another branch snapped to their side, and Maddox ran a hand down her arm, calming her.

It took all in her power not to rub up against him in response. Her wolf whimpered for a moment then stood at attention, ready for whatever was coming for them. She couldn't sense another wolf. No, it was something danger-ous, but something different...

"Caym..." she whispered.

The demon walked out of the trees alone, a smile on his angelic face that looked as if it had been carved in stone. She held back the shudder that threatened to consume her. He was no angel.

She knew more than most just how much of a devil he was.

"I see the three of you are all by yourselves," Caym drawled.

Maddox growled beside her, and she reached out involuntarily, tangling her fingers with his, willing him to not attack. There was no way they'd win against a demon, not with their fists.

"What do you want, Caym?" North asked, his tone cooler than she'd thought possible.

"Your deaths would be appropriate, but I think not yet. No, I want to see the three of you in pain, writhing from the cuts and gashes that I can inflict. Then, when you're just about to heal, I want you to watch your loved ones die screaming your name. You've already left your Pack alone, and they're waiting for me."

"You can't touch them," she said, her voice shaky, but stronger than she'd hoped.

Caym tilted his head, his dark eyes seeming to reach into her soul and violate her all over again. She swallowed the bile that rose into her throat, and Maddox squeezed her hand, again infusing that calming strength she needed.

"Oh, that bitch of mine might have strengthened the wards so I can't come into your precious little den, but that won't stop me for long." Caym smiled, his too-white teeth gleaming. "Ah, but I think you already know that. Tell me, how are Larissa and Neil?"

Maddox growled but didn't move forward. She knew

Caym was just baiting them, enjoying the game as much as he enjoyed anything.

North stood frozen by her side, and she could tell from the energy radiating off him that he too was ready to jump like a spring and attack—even if it did no good.

"No one is going to speak back?" Caym asked, a put-out frown on his face. "I'd hoped for something more from the three of you, though I really shouldn't have. After all, you're just the broken shell of a man, the twin who means nothing, and the whore who spread her legs for me."

Caym grinned, and Ellie's vision blackened for a moment.

Oh, God, he'd said it. He'd told Maddox and North.

Humiliation coated her as she forced herself not to look at either of them. They'd leave her right there where she stood. She'd always known she wasn't good enough, but now she'd lose it all.

Maddox squeezed her hand once more, and she held on for dear life.

Please, don't leave me.

Caym sighed. "You three are boring, honestly. I expected so much more from you. No matter." With that, Caym moved, attacking with a speed she'd hoped to never see again.

North howled beside her, lashing out with hands that had turned to claws. He raked them along Caym's side, and the demon yelled, blood staining his crisp white shirt. Maddox pulled her behind him, going at Caym with his own claws. Ellie growled and waited for another attack, not knowing if Caym was alone.

She'd only be in the way if she attacked Caym. North and Maddox moved like a team, twins born with a bond so close that it would fracture like a thousand pieces of glass when it broke.

Caym might have been faster than either of them, but Maddox and North could still fight on their own, using each other to distract the demon as they attacked. Ellie looked around, pushing out her senses, trying to feel for another enemy. She knew Caym was strong on his own, but it made no sense that he'd come alone when he had an army in his grasp.

She heard the growl before the wolf attacked, and she turned to get out of the way. Two wolves jumped out of the shadows, their teeth bared, and their sickly sweet scent that had been tainted by Caym's evil was cloying.

They came at her at once, and she struck out, using her claws to take them down. They were weaker than her, not only in the sense of hierarchy, but in strength, as well. She ducked and rolled as one of them came at her throat, and the wolf hit the ground with a yelp. Out of the corner of her eye, she saw Maddox and North in their battle with Caym. She couldn't tell if the demon was just waiting for his turn to kill them or if the twins were actually gaining some advantage.

Caym laughed, distracting her, and the other wolf jumped on her, bringing her to the ground. She struggled beneath its weight, turning side to side to avoid its teeth. She kicked and connected with the other wolf that had joined his friend, causing the bastard to yelp in pain.

She heard a growl as the wolf was pulled from her body, and she rolled to her feet, ready to fight. Caym was nowhere to be seen, and North was in the process of killing the wolf she'd kicked.

Maddox yelled as the wolf that had been on top of her slashed his shoulder with its claws. Ellie ran toward them and wrapped her arms around the wolf's neck, squeezing as hard as she could. The wolf struggled against her, and Maddox grabbed the wolf's jaws, pulling them apart until Ellie heard a crack and a snap.

The wolf fell limp in her hold, and she dropped the body to the ground.

Her chest heaved as she looked at Maddox. Blood ran down his shoulder, and she leaned to pull him into a hug. She didn't care if he didn't want it. She *needed* it, and it was about time she did something for herself.

Maddox wrapped his good arm around her, and she inhaled his scent, needing it to wash over her and make sure he was all right.

"We need to take care of that wound, Maddox," she said against his chest, not wanting to let go. "Where did Caym go?"

North walked to their side and shook his head. "Bastard left when you hit the ground. He was just toying with us. I need to make sure there aren't other wolves around. I'm going to leave you two here. Ellie, make sure that wound is cleaned, and I'll take care of it when I get back." North loped off toward the shadows, leaving her in Maddox's arms, the scent of his blood filling her nose.

"Come on, let me take a look at that," she said as she pulled him to a nearby tree.

"I'm fine," he grumbled, and she shook her head.

"No, you're not. You will be, but I want to make sure it's at least clean. We don't know what those guys have under their claws."

Maddox mumbled something she couldn't hear, but he followed her lead. She pushed down on his good shoulder, and he sat on the ground so she could see his wound better.

She held back a wince at the angry, bleeding gashes. There were only two deep ones and one shallow one, and Ellie knew it could have been worse, but that didn't make these any less dangerous.

She rummaged through her bag and found the first aid kit so she could clean them out. Without meeting his gaze, wordlessly, she cleaned out the wound and put a bandage on it. North might have done more or put in stiches, but they didn't have time, and she didn't have the skill.

"How does that feel?"

Maddox groaned, and she met his gaze, afraid she'd hurt him. Instead, she found his gold-rimmed eyes filled with something close to pain, but she didn't think it was from the wound.

"What is it?" she asked.

"Nothing," he whispered.

She risked her heart and placed her palm on his scarred cheek. He pulled away as if she'd scalded him but then leaned into her touch.

Her heart leapt into her throat at the touch that she knew meant more than any other casual graze he'd given her before.

"Thank you for saving my life," she whispered, her hand still on his cheek. Goddess, she never wanted to leave his touch.

Maddox closed his eyes and swallowed hard. "Anything, Ellie. Anything for you."

She sat stunned, not knowing what to say. She ran her hand along his cheek again, feeling every ridge and gash of his scar.

The pain that he held resulting from the scar was more than skin deep, and she didn't know how he'd received it and why it hadn't healed.

Whatever the story was, it had to have been painful, something he'd never shared.

Maybe one day he'd share with her.

Maybe one day.

5

Over Sixty Years Ago.

Maddox washed off the last of the shaving cream from his face and grinned in the mirror. Today was going to be a great day; he could already feel it. His family would be celebrating his and North's birthday that night so he'd get to party with them and still enjoy himself. Yeah, the happiness might be too much for him sometimes, but he'd get over it.

There were things worth the overwhelming feelings in life—like watching his twin laugh when one of his brothers did something to them to make them feel like idiots.

He and North looked alike in every way, even though they were completely different. They each smiled and laughed with the others, but he knew they both had darker sides.

It was the twin thing he guessed.

Before their party, however, he had to go outside the den to help a fellow Pack mate with something. Henry was opening a new store out in the human world and was a little anxious about it. Usually things like that fell under Jasper's job as the Beta, but Maddox thought this might be better suited for it as the Omega. Henry had all the details taken care of, and Jasper had even helped with some of them, but the anxiety of stepping out on his own and dealing with humans on a daily basis fell under Maddox's domain.

He'd help his friend get situated then come back to the den and enjoy time with his family.

Yes, today would be a good day.

He made his way to his car and drove outside the den walls. The trees reached up to the sky, the forest scents infusing him with strength. He loved being a wolf, even if being the Omega was a little too much sometimes. As he aged, so did his powers, meaning with each year, he'd be able to feel more and more. He only hoped he'd be able to handle it all later.

He'd just driven past another checkpoint when he came upon a fallen tree in the middle of the road. He pulled over to the side and got out, trying to figure out what to do. He could go back and get one of his brothers or the enforcers to help him move it, or he could try to do it by himself.

What he didn't know was why the tree fell down in the first place. There hadn't been a storm recently, and as far as he knew, there hadn't been any fights or anything that could have caused it. Cautiously, he walked to the end of the tree to look at its roots and cursed.

Someone had cut it down, blocking the road.

But why?

He heard a branch crack under a footstep, and he turned, ready to fight.

Something hit him on the back of the head, and darkness overcame him before he could lash out.

Hell, it was supposed to be a good day.

He awoke to someone standing over him in a mostly darkened room, illuminated by only a bare bulb.

"Are you sure this is North?" the man above him spat. "How the fuck are you supposed to tell?"

Another man walked to his side. He looked like the other man, and from their power signatures, Maddox had a pretty good idea who they were.

Hector and Corbin, Alpha and Heir to the Central Pack.

Why the hell did they want him?

No, not him. They wanted his twin, North. He and North looked so much alike that even their parents had a tough time telling them apart without sensing their wolves.

"I don't know," the older one, Hector, said. "My contacts said the doctor would be leaving the den to check on a patient. This one must be him. Tell me, boy, I know you're awake, are you North? Or are you the useless one, Maddox?"

Maddox bit back the angry retort. He wasn't useless, but he wasn't about to get in a fighting match with these wolves. They had him at a disadvantage. Not only were there two of them, plus countless others in their Pack if they were indeed in the Central's den, but they'd also chained him to a table with chains strong enough to hold a werewolf in.

Fear crept up his belly, but he didn't show it—couldn't show it.

"I'm North," he lied. There was no way he'd let them know they'd gotten the wrong twin. Yeah, they'd probably kill him anyway, but he wouldn't let North get hurt. He'd protect his twin at all costs.

Corbin grinned. "Finally, something good."

"Why did you take me?" Maddox wasn't sure they'd answer him, but if he got out—no, when—he needed to make sure his family was safe.

They were all that mattered.

"You, North, will be an issue later, so we're going to make sure that doesn't happen," Hector drawled as he walked to the door. "Our elder is a seer and had a vision that you'd be the one to end my boy here." Hector narrowed his eyes. "There's no way I'll let that happen, you see. Corbin is the Heir to this Pack and will not be killed by a fucking Jamenson. You're going to die today, son, but first Corbin is going to make sure it hurts. My son is special that way."

Hector left the room, locking the door behind him, and Maddox growled.

"You kill me and you're starting a war." Maddox fought

at his restraints, knowing it might be useless. His wolf growled and clawed at him, hating being weak.

"They'll never know it was me. Those wolves that took you weren't ours. We hired them, and now, they're dead. There's no trail."

Maddox narrowed his eyes. There was always a trail, and one of his brothers would find it.

Corbin grinned again, sending a shudder down Maddox's spine. He'd deal with anything the bastard brought as long as it meant North was safe.

He had to find a way out of the room, but he knew that wouldn't happen with Corbin by his side. Maybe once the other wolf took a break, Maddox would find a way.

Corbin turned to pick something up from a tray, and Maddox closed his eyes, knowing what was to come would hurt like nothing he'd ever felt.

Corbin cut deep into Maddox's legs, side, and arms using a small knife, and laughing as he did it. Maddox felt fiery agony rip up his body, but he didn't scream out. There was no way he'd give Corbin the satisfaction.

"You're not screaming," Corbin complained with a frown. "I suppose I'll have to use a different knife." He pulled a new one out, and Maddox bit back a groan. "This one was dipped using a special spell, so it will hurt more. It's one of my favorites, so I hope you don't disappoint me. I hate to be disappointed. First, though, I'm going to have you turned over so I can get to your back."

Corbin moved to the door and brought two men in

before Maddox had a chance to move and test the restraints. His cuts bled, and the trails of red stained his clothes and the floor from what he could see, but there was nothing he could do.

He was helpless.

The two wolves, both of whom were built like tanks, moved him to his stomach, and he fought against their hold because they'd loosened the chains to do so. They squeezed his arms, digging into his cuts, and he grunted, trying to break free.

They chained him back down again, the metal links digging into his skin.

"Yes, keep fighting, I like that," Corbin crooned from behind him.

Maddox's wolf whimpered then growled at their position on the table. There was no way to see where Corbin was coming from...no way to protect himself.

The dagger sliced through his skin, and he groaned, holding back the scream that threatened to break free. This cut burned more than the rest, the spell wrapping itself around his body, choking him.

"Finally, a sound out of you, North," Corbin said, pleasure in his tone as he cut deeper slashes along Maddox's back.

At the sound of North's name, Maddox gritted his teeth and bore down. This was for his brother; he had to remember that.

Maddox closed his eyes and drew inward, letting the

pain wash over him as sweat rolled down his back. Corbin cut and sliced while Maddox tried to ignore it.

There had to be a way out.

Finally, he heard Corbin say something else, and then Maddox felt arms around him again, moving him to his back. He tried to fight to free himself, but with the spell and the loss of blood, he was in too much agony to do much. His body felt weak and his limbs heavy, but he tried to get away, to no avail.

They chained him back down, this time tying his head to the table so he couldn't move it. Corbin stood above him, this time with a new dagger in his hand.

"You've done remarkably well, despite how much I'd hoped for the latter. Before I kill you, though, I have a new toy I want to try. I'm going to use it later on my toy, but first I want to see if it works. You see, it's a special one that seals the wounds automatically. I know that doesn't make sense, but you'll understand when you see the final result. It scores the skin and bones so they can't heal correctly, so it will leave the worst scars possible. As much as I love pain, I love seeing the scars and memories more. Let's see how this goes."

Corbin pressed the tip of the blade under Maddox's right eye, and Maddox froze.

Fuck.

"Yes, I think a scar on your face before I kill you will work out perfectly. There's no way I'll let you kill me later.

Oh, I will say that this will hurt more than the other blade. At least that's what my witch told me. We'll see."

Maddox braced himself as Corbin pressed deeper, slicing his skin, and he screamed. He'd been so strong before, but now, he couldn't hold back. He screamed until his throat was raw and his voice cracked. Corbin didn't stop. He just smiled and continued cutting. Maddox could feel fire arch along the cut, searing his skin as it went, scaring him for life.

However long that life would be.

Blood poured out of the wound before it healed, filling his eyes, nose, and mouth. He choked on it, trying to breathe, trying to live.

Maddox felt Corbin pull back, relief and fear filling him.

"I'm going to let you stay here like this until I feel like killing you, North Jamenson. Thank you for showing me what my new dagger can do. Ellie should enjoy it."

Maddox didn't know who Ellie was, but he was sure as hell sorry for her. He didn't want anyone to go through what he'd just gone through...what he was still going through.

He couldn't see with the blood blurring his vision, but he could still use his dulled senses to figure out what to do. He was alone in the room, but weakened beyond reality and chained to a table. He pulled at his chains, trying to get free, but it was no use.

Unless Corbin unchained him to kill him, Maddox would die in his brother's place without his family knowing what had happened to him.

Adam had to be feeling something as the Enforcer since someone outside the Pack had done this, but without evidence, there might not be a trail.

He could only hope they'd find a way to find him before it was too late.

Maddox heard the door open, and he braced himself for what was to come.

This was it.

"Are you alive?" a small feminine voice asked, her voice a fear-filled whisper.

Was it a trick? Was she there to give him hope before Corbin killed him?

He didn't say anything but felt a small hand on his chest.

"I can feel your heart," she whispered. "I can get you unchained and maybe even across the border, but you'll have to get home on your own. I don't want Corbin to find out." The last words broke her voice, as her fear became a tangible thing, heavy in the air.

Maddox couldn't scent her, couldn't see her. He only knew she was someone who was either lying or someone who could give him hope. She had to be a teenager or someone young enough not to pose a threat to his wolf.

The dagger's magic seemed to have taken his wolf's strength as well because his wolf didn't even speak to him, didn't even move to help him.

At this point, he didn't have much choice. He had to trust the girl.

He gave a nod that sent pain down his back and face. He

felt her small hands on the chains as she unlocked them. How she'd gotten the key, he didn't know, but he'd get out of there no matter what.

Once he was free of his chains, he pulled himself up, the cuts ripping open again as they'd begun to heal. Bile rose in his throat as he fought the pain that threatened to overtake him. She put her small body against his, under his armpit, and they made their way out the door and down a hall.

His feet barely held him up, but he didn't want to put too much pressure on her.

He couldn't sense any other wolves around and was grateful for that, even though he wasn't sure why he couldn't. He still couldn't see or smell the way he should, not with the spell working on him and the blood still filling his pores.

"This is as far as I can get you," she said after they'd walked for twenty agonizing minutes. "We're at the border. I know you can't see, but keep going for another hundred feet or so, and you'll find the road. I'm sorry."

"Tell me your name," he whispered, needing to know who had saved him.

"I can't. Go, please, before they find out."

He moved away, taking painful steps the way she'd told him. He heard her running the other way, presumably back to her safe spot in the den. At least he hoped so.

He'd made his way to the road when he heard the scream, a young girl's excruciating scream of terror as she screamed for whoever was hurting her to stop.

Oh, hell, it was her.

Her screams cut off abruptly, and Maddox bent over to throw up.

He'd killed her.

She'd helped him, and his own helplessness had killed his savior.

There was no way he could go back and try to help her... it was too late.

She'd died saving him, and he'd never forget that.

Just as he'd never forget Corbin's promises. North would always be in danger as long as Corbin was alive. There had to be a way to protect his family. He touched the newly formed scar on his face.

There would be no chance of mistaking one twin for another now.

That meant Corbin might try again, but not if Maddox had anything to say about it. Maddox and North would always have to look over their shoulders for danger.

Maddox vowed to protect his brother at all cost, even hiding who'd done this to him. If he told his family, they'd start a war, and he couldn't risk his family.

No, this would be his secret.

His burden.

Anything for his family.

Anything for North.

Anything for the girl who'd saved his life and lost hers in the process.

He wouldn't let her die in vain.

He'd have to make sure he was worth something. He would have to make sure he was worth that girl's sacrifice. He couldn't be the man he was before; that man was long gone.

He was the Omega.

He'd protect them all.

6

P resent Day

Maddox pressed his hand to his cheek, letting his fingers trace the scar that had been a part of his life for so long that he almost didn't remember what it was like to not have it.

Almost.

He blinked away the memories of his screams and the girl who had died for him. Countless times he'd almost asked Ellie who she'd been, if Ellie had known the girl who had saved him, but he'd stopped himself in time. He hadn't wanted to face the memories or the curious looks.

He was pretty sure Ellie didn't know he'd been in the Central's den as their prisoner, and he didn't want to change that. No one except his enemies knew how he'd received his scar, and he wouldn't change that. He couldn't burden his family.

Corbin had learned that he'd gotten the wrong twin. Tales of the scarred Omega had reached out far beyond the borders of the Redwood Pack and the legend of how he'd received such a horrific injury grew in falsehoods with each passing year. By the time Corbin had learned it was, in fact, Maddox, not North, who had almost died, too much time had passed to do anything about it. Corbin had been lying in wait for North, and Maddox wouldn't let anything happen to his twin.

He'd do anything for his twin...even if North had the one thing Maddox so desperately wanted yet could never have.

Maddox had done his best to stop his family from hovering over him. They'd all wanted to know what happened, but he hadn't told them. As Alpha, his father had even ordered him to tell, and Maddox had disobeyed. The pain to his wolf and fighting the bond between him and his father had been almost as agonizing as the cut, but he had to keep it a secret.

He hadn't wanted his family to be in danger.

His mother had scolded his father for using the magic against him, and his family hadn't asked since, as if they'd finally known he wouldn't say anything—couldn't say anything.

He'd been right though.

He wasn't the same man he'd been before his scar.

The bond between him and his Pack seemed to have been turned on full blast since then, and his powers had increased to the point of pain. Instead of a steady increase over time, where he'd have been able to gradually learn to handle it, instead, he'd had to deal with it all at once.

And people wondered why he'd rather be alone most days.

"Maddox?" Ellie asked from his side, pulling him out of his thoughts.

They'd moved to a new location after North had come back letting them know he hadn't found any other wolves or Caym around. By then, Ellie had walked away to keep guard. She hadn't even let him stand by her side as she said she'd rather him heal.

His wolf had liked that she'd wanted to take care of him while he'd have rather run and dealt with other things.

Anything other than the feelings that were spreading through him.

She was North's.

Not his.

He needed to get that through his thick skull.

"Maddox?" Ellie asked again and ran a hand down his arm.

He pulled back as if she'd burned him, not liking the way he craved her touch, her scent and everything about her.

It had been hell to stay away from his mate when they'd been within the den. Now, it was pure torture.

"What?" he snapped then closed his eyes. He needed to stop yelling at her for every single thing, but he couldn't help it. She had him on edge and wouldn't leave his side. She should be by North, not sitting by him so he could scent that sweet wolf that his wolf wanted so much.

"You're lost in thought, and we're not in the best place to do that," she said, her voice low but filled with annoyance.

Good. She should be annoyed with him. At least she was learning to fight back; although, he didn't see her do it with anyone else. Figured he'd be the one she could feel safe yelling at.

"You're right," he said after tearing his gaze from hers. "I can smell the rain coming, and we still have a long hike to that cabin."

Maddox moved to get up, and Ellie put her hand on his side, helping him. He froze at the movement, almost toppling them over. He righted himself and winced as the cut on his shoulder pulled.

"Are you okay?" Ellie asked, concern in her gaze as she ran a hand up his side to the bandage.

He pulled back, afraid of her touch. She needed to stop doing that. They'd gone so long not talking and touching, and yet when he'd pulled her behind him to protect her from his own Pack, it had opened a floodgate. He needed to close it immediately.

It would only hurt the both of them—and North—the longer he let it continue.

Maddox pulled away from her touch, ignoring the hurt in her eyes. It was for the best.

"It's fine. I'm healing." He moved past, careful not to

brush against her. "Thanks for helping," he added, unable to be the complete ass he needed to be.

"Where exactly is this cabin?" she asked as her steps fell in synch with his.

"Not too far, but we need to get there before the storm. I'm not in the mood to deal with that on top of the tension in the air."

"Tension? You mean the Centrals, or what's going on with the three of us?"

He looked over at her sharply and tripped over a root.

"Fuck," he said as he found his footing again. "Just go away, Ellie." Please, for both our sakes. "I already told you we aren't going to be mates, so just leave. I'll get you to the cabin and make sure the Centrals won't hurt you. Only because you're Pack," he lied, hating himself. His wolf clawed at him, growling, but he ignored it.

She blanched, but she shook her head. "Not good enough, Maddox. Not good enough by far."

She walked away from him, her back straight and her shoulders stiff.

God, he was an ass.

No, he was worse. He'd hurt the one person he could love, yet he'd had to. He needed her to stay away so she could be happy. She didn't deserve what he'd bring to her through their bond.

It was too much.

"I always knew you could be hard if you had to be, but I never knew you'd be so cruel."

Maddox didn't look toward North, knowing the disappointment on his twin's face would be too much to handle.

"She'll be fine," Maddox said, willing it to happen.

"You're an idiot, a fucking idiot."

"You don't understand, North. Plus, I thought you'd be happy with this whole development."

If North didn't form a bond with Ellie...well, Maddox didn't know what he'd do. The thought of them actually mating, though, made him sick to his stomach.

The fates surely hated him. Omegas weren't supposed to mate. They were supposed to die alone and in pain and not able to burden others with their so-called gifts.

That's the way it had always been, and he wasn't about to change that.

Lightning arched across the sky, and Maddox held back a shiver. The gods seemed to have opened a faucet, and the clouds burst, rain pelting them in heavy sheets, causing their coats to drench and everything else to stick to their skin.

"We need to get to shelter!" Maddox yelled over the wind and rain as he ran to Ellie's side. She didn't know the way, only the general direction, so he needed to be the one who led.

"Maddox, wait up," North shouted as he jogged toward them. "What the hell did you mean back there?"

Maddox looked at his brother as if he'd lost his mind. Really? Like this was the best time to talk about this shit?

"We need to get to the cabin or at least somewhere

where we don't get drenched more than we are," Maddox said over the wind as he picked up his pace, Ellie by his side.

"No, we're going to get this out in the open now," North argued even as he kept up his stride.

"You're kidding, right?" Maddox shook his head, trying to get the rain out of his eyes. "We need to get out of here."

"What did you mean that I should be happy that you're treating Ellie like shit?" North asked, his eyes glowing gold as his voice shook with what could only be anger.

"North, let it go," Ellie said, and Maddox whipped his head around to look at her.

"Finally, some sense. Let's get going." He sped up, practically running through the forest as the rain pelted him.

He didn't want to have this conversation ever—even if his father had decreed it. They'd have their words, and then North would leave with Ellie, finally able to be her protector and mate. Maddox would stay behind and watch it happen. He'd watched the rest of his brothers mate one by one, having to deal with every single ounce of happiness, angst, and pain that went with falling in love, and he was so fucking happy he wouldn't have to feel it with North and Ellie.

He'd never have to feel their happiness, their joy, their elation...none of it.

Oh, he'd have to sit back and watch it and pretend everything was okay even when he wanted to jump off a cliff, but he'd deal with it.

He always had in the past, and he wouldn't stop now.

He ignored North's and Ellie's shouts from behind him, though he knew they were running, trying to keep up.

"Maddox, stop running away from us," North bellowed. "Dad told us to deal with this, and yeah, the rain sucks, but we can't keep going on like we are."

Maddox stopped, his chest heaving, not from the exertion, but from his own desire not to do this. He couldn't tell Ellie what he felt, and he damn well couldn't tell North.

It wasn't as if he'd done such a remarkable job hiding it recently anyway.

He didn't turn because he couldn't stomach looking at them. They'd be perfect for each other. Ellie deserved the unblemished twin, the one who could help her heal with his grace and ability to aid those in need.

Maddox couldn't help her...he wasn't worthy enough.

Why else would the fates block her emotions from him?

"Maddox," Ellie said, her voice low but loud enough to be heard over the storm.

God, he wanted to hear her say his name in the heat of passion when he'd lay her down and fill her so she'd be his. He wanted to make sure she forgot everything that had ever happened to her at the hands of her brother and the demon that was a blight on this plane.

He wanted to be the one who held her when she broke and helped her heal the fractures that never seemed to heal with words alone.

He wanted to be the one who filled her belly with their child and watched her grow round.

He wanted to be the one who made her smile, made her laugh, made her everything she wanted to be.

Maddox swallowed hard. No, that couldn't be him.

He'd been foolish to think that it could be.

Maybe if North hadn't also been her mate, he would have been able to find a way, but when she had a perfectly good choice that wouldn't break her, he didn't stand a chance. There was no other reason that North and Ellie had taken to each other so well. They had to be mates.

He couldn't take that chance.

"Maddox," Ellie repeated. "Just talk to us, talk to me. We'll get out of the storm soon, but can't you see that you're hurting us and yourself?"

Maddox closed his eyes and let her words wash over him. "We need to go," he said, his words vacant.

"Talk to us, Mad," North said as he placed his hand on Maddox's uninjured shoulder.

"You two are going to be fine. I'll deal with everything on the outside to make sure nothing happens to you, but leave me be."

Let me be alone.

"What are you talking about?" Ellie asked.

Maddox gave a hollow chuckle. "You two can go and mate and live happily ever after. Stop waiting around to see what I will do. I know you're not bonded yet because you're afraid you'll hurt me, but you're only hurting each other. Cement that bond and be together. I'm fine with it."

Ellie gasped, and he turned to her, not able to hold back. Though the rain was hitting them in sheets, he could tell the tracks of rain running down her cheeks were mixed with tears.

"How...how could you think that?" she asked, her voice shaking.

"I see the way you two are together," he said, ready to get it all out in the open so they could leave and he could find whatever semblance of peace possible.

"No, you don't," Elle argued, her voice heating. "You don't see anything. I can't believe you'd think I'd do that. How could your wolf even think that? I knew you were pulling away for some reason, but I never thought it was because you thought I'd want anyone else but you. God, can't you see we're supposed to bond? I don't get how you could do this." She ran past him in the direction of the cabin, and he stood frozen.

"Ellie!" North yelled. "Stay where you are. We don't want to split up, even if my brother is a fucking idiot."

Ellie stopped about twenty feet head of them, her shoulders shaking.

North turned toward Maddox and punched him in the face. Pain ricocheted in his cheek, and Maddox cursed, spitting out blood.

"What the fuck?"

"Why the hell didn't you say anything?" North asked.

"I thought it was obvious."

Hadn't it been?

"Ellie isn't my mate."

"What? No, you're wrong. I've seen the way you two are. You're always together. I stood back because you two need each other."

No, North had to be wrong.

North shook his head. "We'll get back to your actions in a minute. She's yours, Mad. My wolf feels for her."

Maddox growled. Hell, he'd been saying the same thing for months, but he didn't need to hear it from North. His brother had just said Ellie wasn't his mate, and now, he claimed his wolf had feelings for her?

What the hell?

North held up his hands. "No, not that way. My wolf wants to make sure she's protected, warm, while your wolf heals. He knows that you're her mate and that you need her. But he doesn't want her to be alone."

"I don't understand," he whispered over the wind, though his brother was close enough that he'd have heard him.

Ellie wasn't North's?

What did that mean?

North have a hollow laugh. "We're connected, Mad. We're brothers, twins, two halves of a whole. I can't be happy unless you are. Your happiness lies within Ellie, and I can't sit back and watch the two of you hurt each other. That's why I was there. That's why I took her under my wing. Not because I loved her like you should or do, but because she makes you a better wolf."

"North..." Maddox didn't know what to say, what to do.

He'd just been thinking that if North hadn't been with Ellie he would have tried to make it work, but was that really true?

Fuck, nothing made sense.

"Mad, just shut up. We'll get to the cabin, and you and Ellie can talk—something we all should have done long before this. You're going to have to deal with whatever shit is going on in your head because you've hurt that girl over there. Yes, she can hear us. She knows what's going on, so get the fuck over yourself."

Maddox let out a breath, and no words came to mind.

"Talk to her, Mad. Tell her why you think you can't mate her because I sure as hell know all this shit you're putting us through isn't just because you think I'm in the way. Something else is hiding beneath the surface, and you just need to get it out."

North left him standing in the rain and ran to Ellie's side. She didn't look at his brother, but rather she met Maddox's gaze, her dark eyes filled with something he couldn't recognize...hope?

No, it couldn't be that.

He'd broken that...hadn't he?

Nothing made sense anymore...nothing.

7

M addox thought she was North's mate?

Ellie couldn't believe it. He'd never said anything like that. Never.

All this time...lost...because of a misconception. That didn't make any sense. There had to be something more to that. He wouldn't have pushed her away without giving her the choice, would he?

For North...he just might have.

Goddess, none of this made sense. Her wolf whimpered at Ellie's confusion, and Ellie wanted to break down with her—not that she'd do that.

They were getting close to the cabin according to North, and she couldn't wait to get out of her wet clothes—alone.

The thought of Maddox wrapped around her as they bonded filled her mind and made her want to weep. She didn't want to think about how his skin would feel heated against hers, how his calloused fingertips would trail along her body, sending shivers in their wake.

She'd never had a night like that... She'd only felt pain where there should have been caresses.

Now that Maddox knew that North wasn't hers, the question was what he'd do with that.

What if she *still* wasn't good enough?

She'd been told that her entire life, and even though the Jamensons had tried to show her she had value, she couldn't quite believe them.

They walked another mile or so, and the rain let up, as if it had only stormed to show the depth of their pain, their cluelessness.

"Ellie," North whispered as he came to her side, "I'm sorry you had to hear that, but it needed to be said."

She shrugged, not really in the mood to talk to him. No, her damned self wanted to talk to Maddox—the wolf who wanted nothing to do with her.

Great going, Ellie.

"Ellie, talk to me," North implored. "You know you can always talk to me."

"I can't, North." She stopped and ran her hands through her too-long hair. It ran down to the middle of her back, and she hated it. It was something Corbin had loved, and he'd never let her cut it.

She'd almost cut it once then she'd seen the way Maddox had looked at, and she'd kept it.

God, why couldn't she just do something for herself for once?

She hated that she didn't know anything, and that was why she was living in this cycle of self-doubt and pain. North had gotten at least part of the story out of Maddox, but it was damn time she got the rest from the wolf who didn't want her.

"Why can't you, Ellie?" He reached out to hold her hand like he always did when he was trying to help her, and she pulled away, aware Maddox was watching them.

The Pack had always watched her, as if they'd been afraid she'd turn on them at any moment. Considering where they were, and *why* they were there, it made sense, but she'd always known when one of those gazes was Maddox's.

His was different.

It wasn't filled with fear or contempt that made the fear crawl in her belly and threaten to take hold. No, his gaze was a slow burn that was mixed with the unknown and something she so desperately wanted to be a promise.

She just didn't know anymore.

"Thank you so much for helping me, North, but you need to give me some space," she whispered. "You understand, don't you?"

North gave her a sad smile and nodded. "It'll all work out, don't worry."

She tried to smile back, but failed. She didn't quite

believe it, but she'd go with it just to keep moving. They had to be approaching the cabin soon.

"What is this place again?" Ellie asked, expecting North to answer and was surprised that Maddox did instead.

"It's a cabin owned by my family, but not in the den."

"You guys can have places outside the den?" She didn't know how normal Packs worked considering where she'd grown up. The Redwoods had been a revelation in more ways than one.

"Sure, Kade and Jasper own their own business that's not for Pack only, but for humans and other wolves and witches as well. A lot of us do, actually. It's hard to find a way to create an income within our own society, so we need the outside world to help us. With the war going on, though, we've been forced to put a lot of that on hold. Kade and Jasper's business is being run by their assistants at the moment because they can't leave the den for longer than necessary."

She couldn't believe he'd spoken that much to her about anything, let alone something about the way the den worked. He'd always been so closed off from her. She couldn't tell if this sudden change was because of their close proximity due to the danger surrounding them or North's earlier declaration.

Either way, she'd take it.

Well, she'd take it after he figured out what the hell he wanted and apologize to her.

Yes, she needed that too because she needed to heal.

Lying back and being beaten verbally as well as physically was in her past.

It was time to move on.

"So, no one is in this cabin now?" she asked.

Maddox shook his head, and she had to hold herself back from running her hand through those dirty blond locks. She knew it was partly because of the mating urge riding her, but the human in her wanted this man, as well.

There was just something beyond his wolf that called to her.

"Shouldn't be. It's a Jamenson holding, not the Pack's, and considering all of us are either right here or back at the den, it should be empty."

"And we'll be safe there?"

Safety...goddess she wanted that word to mean something beyond being pain-free.

"I'll keep you safe, Ellie," Maddox whispered, and Ellie had to turn her head away from him, afraid he'd see too much of her.

He's said *I* not *we*.

That had to mean something.

Right?

They made their way toward the cabin, and North froze, his shoulders stiffening.

"What is it?" Ellie whispered and pushed out her senses, trying to find evidence of the Centrals.

"We're not alone," Maddox whispered as he pulled her

closer to his side. Heat radiated off him, calming her ever so slightly, even as the tension grew heavy in the air.

A wolf slid out of the bushes, his back arched, ready to pounce. His fur was dark, almost black, his eyes glowing gold around a hazel iris. He didn't look tainted like the Centrals. No, he looked like a wolf defending his territory. Ellie took in a deep breath, not recognizing the scent, but knowing it was a werewolf, not a wild animal.

What was he doing out here all alone?

Ellie tore her gaze from the wolf, trusting the men to watch him. She searched the surrounding trees for movement. It was highly doubtful he was alone—especially with their luck.

North growled and flexed his hands, his claws shifting. He took a step toward the wolf, his power washing over them all. Even though North wasn't the Alpha, he was still higher in ranking than almost all of the wolves in the Pack. In fact, other than Edward and Kade, Ellie wasn't even sure who ranked next on a daily basis. They seemed to have their own fragile hold on a hierarchy that worked for them.

This wolf, however, was not part of that, and just the feel of his power set Ellie on edge.

This was *not* a submissive wolf.

In fact, Ellie wasn't even sure he was lower in power than Maddox and North. This couldn't end well, not unless they used words instead of teeth and claws. It didn't matter, though, because, below it all, they still held the spirit of an animal, and sometimes words were not enough—much to her dismay.

Maddox pulled her to his side, a subtle move that gave her a bare wisp of his scent. She might have been trained, but she was still the weak link in this game.

The other wolf growled again, his head low, looking ready to pounce at any moment. North stood in front of her and Maddox, the power play not ending any time soon.

Then the wolf jumped, his teeth bared. North turned and lowered his shoulder and rammed into the wolf's flank, sending them both to the ground. North rolled off the wolf and, as he stood, threw off his pack, ripped his clothes from his body and turned.

Hell.

She'd never seen a turn that quick before, not even from the Alpha.

North turned into a gray and tan wolf, as large as the black one he fought with. The attacked each other, teeth and claws digging into each other's flanks as Maddox pulled her to his side.

"Help North," she said over the growls and yips.

"I'm not leaving you alone. North can handle himself. We don't know if he's alone."

"As much as I like you thinking of me, your brother is the one in trouble right now. Plus, I don't think he's a Central."

Maddox shook his head. "I can't smell that tangy scent on him either, but I don't know."

Ellie bit her lip and held herself back from screaming. She didn't want to do anything of the kind. She didn't want to search within herself to see if there was the stain of her old Pack.

She did it anyway though. North and Maddox were more important than her feelings. As it was, the wolves fighting in front of here weren't fighting to the death. No, they seemed to be pulling back, only clawing and biting to discover who was tougher.

She closed her eyes and reached out with her wolf, trying to see if there was anything of the Centrals entwined within the other wolf.

This wolf was a lone wolf, Packless, though he had a taste of something that had once been, as if he'd been part of a Pack before.

"He's not Central. I think he's just defending his territory," she said after she pulled back.

"This is *our* cabin, *our* territory," Maddox growled.

"Yes, but you weren't here, and I think he's a lone wolf, Maddox. Something bad must have happened."

Maddox gripped her tighter, and Ellie shook her head. "We have to stop them. They're just battling for dominance now, and it won't change a thing because all three of you have similar levels of power."

Maddox gave a nod but didn't say anything. Damn, this would be up to her then.

"Stop it, both of you!" she yelled. "We're not settling anything here. Change back and talk it out like men. We're not the animals your behavior is displaying."

Both wolves stopped mid strike and stared at her as though she'd lost her damned mind. Well, maybe she had. After that bout of confidence, she sank into Maddox's hold, afraid of what they'd do to her since she'd mouthed off. Some behaviors couldn't be broken.

Maddox squeezed her, and she looked up. He gave her a slight smile that caused her heart to leap into her throat.

North and the other wolf broke apart, and magic washed over her as they both shifted back. Now, there were two very sexy and *very* naked men standing in front over. Slight nicks and cuts marred their otherwise perfect skin.

North looked just like Maddox—sans scars—but still, he didn't do anything for her. Neither did the other man, who looked like a built god. His thick chest heaved as he breathed hard, his muscles stretching and filling him out nicely. His brown hair was cut short, but still long enough for him to run his fingers though. As she was a wolf, she purposely didn't look below their waists. Not that she didn't want to—she was a woman after all.

They might be nonchalant about nudity in most cases, but that didn't mean she should stare at them.

Maddox pinched her hip, and she looked up at him.

Could that be jealousy on his face?

Well, then.

"Who are you, and why are you on our property?" North asked the other man.

"Your property? You haven't been here in over a year," the other man growled.

"Logan! Stop antagonizing them. Don't you see they're the Redwoods?" A woman with long blond hair and a thin build walked toward them from the cabin that was just near them, a boy of about eight or so behind her. He looked like both Logan and this woman but had tanner skin and shaggy hair. Either he was a brother or their son, Ellie didn't know.

"Lexi, what the hell did I say about coming out here? Go back to the cabin and take Parker with you," Logan growled as he moved back toward her without turning away from North.

Lexi rolled her eyes then stopped when she got a good look at North. Her gaze traveled over him—*all* of him—and she swallowed hard.

Well, then. Interesting.

Maddox walked forward and bent to pick up North's pack. He pulled out some jeans and a shirt and threw them at North.

"Put these on and stop acting like an ass," Maddox ordered then looked toward Logan. "Since it seems you've been living here while we've been at war and away from our cabin, I'd assume you have your own clothes there?"

Logan glared but gave a jerky nod.

Dear Lord, men were stubborn idiots sometimes.

Lexi walked up to them and gave them a smile, though Ellie could see the danger behind it. There was no doubt she'd attack if they posed a threat to Parker.

"You know our names, but not who we are. I understand that. We're no threat to the Redwoods, but I understand you have to be careful, as do we. I'm Lexi, and this is my brother Logan." She gave a nod to her naked brother as he crossed his arms over his chest. "This is my son, Parker." She wrapped an arm around Parker while she said it.

The boy smiled at them, and Ellie frowned. There was something about him she couldn't place...something familiar.

Parker turned to look at North, and Ellie did the same and bit her lip. North looked like someone had punched him in the stomach and then stolen his puppy.

North, now dressed, swallowed hard then gave a slight nod. "Nice to meet you under the circumstances. I'm North, and this, as you can tell, is my brother, Maddox, and our Pack mate, Ellie."

Maddox grabbed her hand and pulled her closer, causing her heart to speed up. Damn wolf.

"Let's head to the cabin then?" Maddox asked, but Ellie could tell it wasn't really a question. "I think there are some things we need to discuss."

They followed the trio and North to the cabin, tension in the air, but this time the tension was one of curiosity, rather than danger. She still didn't trust them, but something told her they had a story to tell and might need help as much as she did.

Maybe she wasn't so alone after all.

8

Maddox sat on the couch in the living room of the small cabin and took in his surroundings. The paint was old but not peeling yet. It had only been a few years since he and his family had been in the place and it had been needing a coat, anyway. Kade and Jasper has mentioned they'd wanted to expand it for their families and let out some of their creativity. Too bad they hadn't been able to do anything but worry about things like the Pack since Caym had come to their plane.

The furniture was old, but comfortable, and since there were so many Jamensons, they had plenty of seating— something that didn't happen in other cabins. His mother had decorated it with her usual homey charm. Pictures adorned the walls, and mirrors had been placed in strategic locations so the place not only looked larger, but they could see their entire surroundings in case of attack. As the place wasn't on den land, they had to be careful.

Neutral wasn't always so neutral.

The place should have had layers of dust and a musty smell, yet all Maddox could sense were these other wolves and North and Ellie. Whoever this family was, they hadn't changed much, as if they'd been ready to leave on a moment's notice.

He'd have to figure out just exactly why that was.

Ellie had said they weren't Centrals, and Maddox knew for a fact they had never been Redwoods. Even banished wolves would still have an echo to his wolf—a bond that would have been broken, but not forgotten. It could be true that these wolves were of another Pack, ousted for one reason or another, but Maddox didn't know.

He'd tasted their scents and knew that, though they were not of a Pack now, that hadn't always been the case. Something had forced them out of their Pack, and Maddox needed to know what it was. Ellie was in danger from these people. Yes, so were he and North, but Ellie was more important.

He still hadn't thought about what North's revelations would mean to his future. Even though she wouldn't mate his brother, that didn't take away the enormity of burdens he'd put on her if they did mate.

He couldn't let that happen to her...yet, without North in the way, it became just that much harder to say no.

"Maddox?" Ellie shifted on the couch so her leg brushed against his, sending heat right to his dick.

Hell, this would be torture until they talked it out fully and probably after that. However, they had more important things to worry about at the moment.

Namely the Centrals and whoever these three were.

"This was unexpected," he said, not even bothering to whisper, as they were in a house full of wolves and hiding their conversation was out of the question.

"I know. I don't know if we're doing the right thing at all, but my wolf feels safe with them, you know?" Ellie whispered.

Safe.

Gods, he wanted her to feel safe. He knew she'd never felt it before, and now everything that she'd built around her was crumbling away with the emergence of a traitor in their Pack.

Maddox nodded and forced himself not to reach for her hand again. For some reason, she settled him and his wolf when he did so, but he couldn't form the habit or get used to it.

She wasn't for him.

He had to remember that, even if it was getting harder and harder to remember why he was saying no, why he was pushing her away.

"We'll figure it all out."

Logan had gone to change into something besides his skin while North sat on the ottoman, waiting for Lexi and

Parker to come from the kitchen. It all seemed so surreal. They'd come to the cabin as a place of refuge to protect themselves, but they hadn't been the first to do the same.

"So, who wants to start?" Lexi asked as she walked in the room, Parker by her side. Logan pushed past her and glared.

"I want to know what they're doing here." Logan went right up to North and stood over him.

North blinked and sat where we was, seemingly unaffected by the show of dominance.

"Logan," Lexi whispered as she shook her head.

"How about we all agree not to go for each other's throats while we figure this out?" Maddox said, wishing he'd be able to use his Omega strength to help. Since these three weren't of Pack, and North and Ellie had no connection to that part of him, he felt useless.

"I thought that's what we'd already decided," Ellie said, and Maddox had to hold back a grin. It seemed as though she was starting to gain a backbone.

Nice.

"We did," Lexi agreed. "Logan, stop it. Okay?"

Logan snorted then went to stand on Lexi's other side.

"How about you guys sit on the other couch?" Ellie asked, and Maddox was glad she'd spoken up. Logan seemed to listen to her more than he and North. Probably because she wasn't trying to tear his throat out. Not that he'd tried, but he'd thought about it. Vividly. "There's plenty of room, and this way no one is standing over anyone else."

Lexi smiled, which brightened her whole face. Not that

she did anything for him. No, the caramel-skinned beauty by his side was the one who did it. If Maddox were to venture a guess, he would say he wasn't the twin Lexi had her eye on. From the look on North's face, the feeling was mutual.

Interesting.

Considering Lexi had a son, that meant she'd had a mate at one time. Wolves couldn't have children unless they were bonded with their mates. Since wolves had more than one predestined mate, it was possible to find another mate in their long lifespans.

His brother, Adam, was a prime example considering he'd lost his mate, Anna, years before and now, was happily mated to Bay. His other brother, Kade, had met Melanie after being rejected by a previous potential mate—one the rest of the family was happy to be rid of.

However, since fate wasn't always so cruel, once a wolf was bonded, they couldn't feel the mating urge with another wolf unless their mate died.

Since it was clear—at least to Maddox—that Lexi and North had at least felt *something*, Lexi's mate and Parker's father must be dead.

That could be a reason they were currently Packless.

"Since this *is* our land, how about we start?" Maddox said after a moment, and Logan gave a curt nod. Considering he didn't know these people and where they stood, Maddox felt it was best to start at the beginning. "You know there's a war between the Centrals and Redwoods, correct?"

"We all know about the Centrals and their demon kind," Logan spat. "They want to be the strongest Pack in the world, so they have to take you down to do it. Too bad they're killing the rest of us in the process."

Maddox growled. "They're killing us as well. Don't forget that."

"Then why aren't you doing something about it?" Logan yelled.

"We are," North cut in. His brother's eyes glowed gold for just a moment before he settled himself. Odd because North was usually the calmest of them all—at least on the outside. Something—or rather some*one*—had to be affecting him pretty badly. "We are, but we can't beat them with their dark magic. We're trying our best, but without tainting ourselves in the process, we're treading water until we find another way."

"And we've found ways to prevent him from coming into our den," Maddox said. He didn't mention Bay and her connection to Caym, nor did he say anything about *why* they were on the run...at least not yet. The Redwoods weren't safe, but, eventually, they would be.

They had to be.

"We've heard you brought the spawn of Caym into your fold," Logan said with a glare.

Maddox's wolf clawed at the surface, but he held him back. "I see you think you know our secrets, but beware of how you talk of our sister-in-law."

If they already knew about what Bay was—or at least

had a glimpse—Maddox had to make sure she was safe, meaning she held their name, their protection.

Logan's brows rose for a moment, and Maddox had to hold back a grin. It seems the wolf didn't know everything he thought he did.

"Can we stop with the posturing, boys?" Lexi asked as she shot a look toward her brother.

"Yes, please," Ellie mumbled and again Maddox had to hold back from taking her hand in his.

"The war is escalating, and there have been losses on both sides," Maddox continued. "Because we've cut him off from our den, he's trying to find new ways of attacking us."

"He must be using his sister then," Lexi said as she gave Ellie a look.

Ellie froze, and he rested his hand on her knee, willing her to stay calm. He didn't know what this Lexi knew, but Ellie would not be harmed because if it.

His wolf growled in agreement.

"I might be of his blood, but that doesn't make me his," Ellie said, her voice hollow, but he knew she wanted to scream, do *something* to take away that part of her.

Lexi lowered her gaze, her wolf the lowest in the hierarchy of the bunch. "I know, Ellie. I *know*."

Ellie sucked in a breath, and Maddox squeezed her knee. How could she know?

"What else do you know, Lexi?" Maddox asked, his tone as calm as possible.

"I know enough," she said, and he had a feeling they'd

get no more of how exactly she knew of Corbin and his...talents.

"I take it you're here then to hide Ellie from her brother," Logan put in, cutting through the tension.

"For now," Maddox said. "Now tell us, what are you doing here?"

"Doing much of the same," Logan answered. "Hiding from those who want us gone from this plane."

"What happened to make you fear for your lives?" Maddox asked. He was very careful not to say anything like *"What did you do?"* because that would only set Logan off again. They didn't have time to deal with this wolf's alpha tendencies.

"We were Talons," Logan supplied, and Maddox nodded.

The Talons were the Pack on the other side of the Centrals. They'd already lost one female wolf when Caym had killed her because she looked like Willow, Jasper's mate, and the woman Caym wanted as his next "project". Maddox wasn't sure what else the Talons had lost in the process. They were also the same Pack that had kicked Bay's mother out when she'd been raped by Caym and forced to breed a half-demon baby.

The Talons weren't high on his list of priorities at the moment because of their Alpha's choices.

"They banished us from the Pack because...because of our lack of choices," Lexi said, and Maddox shook his head.

"That's a little vague," he said.

"That's as detailed as I can be." Her eyes beseeched him, and then she looked down at her son.

Ah, so it was because of Parker, or maybe his dead father.

"The Alpha, Joseph, he just kicked you out?" North asked, anger threading his tone.

"Yes, there was nothing we could do," Lexi answered. "We've been lone wolves for a while. I mean, if you can be a lone wolf in a family."

"They kicked all of you out?" North asked.

Logan growled. "I left on my own. I wouldn't leave Lexi to fend for herself and Parker."

"Family sometimes needs to take priority over Pack," Maddox said. "I understand."

Logan nodded. "Joseph isn't much of an Alpha. He's a lazy prick, sorry, Parker, that relies on his seven sons and princess to take care of the Pack. He meanwhile sits back and takes care of himself so he doesn't die in the battle."

Maddox growled. "An Alpha should protect his Pack."

Logan met his gaze. "Well, like I said, Joseph isn't much of an Alpha."

Hell, the Packs were disintegrating around the Redwoods, and yet they could only focus on the demon. Sometimes the price of war wasn't what could be seen but what was left behind when help wasn't available.

"So, you guys are just nomads until...what?" Ellie asked, her voice filled with more warmth than before. Lexi seem-

ingly knowing some of her past had made her freeze beside
him. He'd have to find a way to help her later.

Damn it, he couldn't do that. Not when he needed to
keep his distance.

"Until we find a way to be safe and stop having to move
around," Lexi said as she hugged Parker close to her.

The boy hadn't said anything since they'd met, but
Maddox didn't blame him. After all, they'd been on the run
for probably most, if not all, of his life, and now he sat in a
room with three strangers, two of them very dominant
wolves and the third a wolf who was just broken enough
that she made most wolves want to take care of her.

"So, what are we going to do then?" Maddox asked,
needing to find a way to calm his wolf and Ellie.

"I don't plan on fighting you," Logan said. "As long as
you don't hurt my family." A lethal edge marred his tone.

"The same for us," North said, just as deadly.

"Why haven't you tried to ask any of the other Packs for
sanctuary?" Maddox asked, needing to know at least one
answer.

"I don't know if we'll be welcome," Lexi whispered.

Maddox let out a breath and ran his hand through his
hair. "Is there a reason for that?" She didn't answer. "We
need to finish our journey, but if things come to it, we can
bring you to our father."

Lexi gave a small smile. "Maybe."

She didn't sound as if she'd believe him. Why would
she? She'd been thrown out of the only family and Pack

she'd ever known—a very painful process. There was no reason for her to trust wolves from another Pack.

Ellie shifted on the couch, running a hand down his arm, and Maddox groaned.

"It's the full moon tonight," he said as his wolf practically rolled its eyes.

"Yes, we're planning on doing a run so Parker can let his wolf out," Logan said.

Since the other man had just shifted, as had North, technically, they wouldn't have needed to let their wolves free tonight. Werewolves weren't governed by the moon, but during the full one, the goddess called to them, and most liked to run during that time when the animal inside them was the strongest.

Maddox looked out at the setting sun and cursed. "I'll have to shift; it's been too long for me."

"Me, too," Ellie whispered.

"I can stay behind and watch the perimeter and make sure things are settled," North offered. "I take it we'll be sharing the same space for a little while."

Logan cocked his head then shrugged. "I'll go with you and Parker then. I don't need to shift, but I'm not sending my nephew out with strangers."

"What about Lexi?" North asked.

She lifted her chin and met his gaze for a moment before breaking it. "I'm latent. I won't be on the hunt with the rest of you."

Maddox's wolf howled at the news.

Dear goddess.

She couldn't shift. Like all wolves, her wolf's soul shared her body with her, but her wolf would be forever trapped, unable to run, be free, and just...be.

It was agony for those involved, and most latent shifters died at a young age.

Lexi must have been submissive enough that her wolf could handle living on two feet rather than four paws. If she'd been any more dominant, she wouldn't have stood a chance.

"Then we'll stay behind and guard the cabin," North said, an odd look in his eyes.

Logan growled and stood again, facing North. "I don't know if I trust you alone with my sister."

North stood this time, not letting the other man have the more dominant position. "Are you suggesting I'd harm a woman?"

Ellie grabbed Maddox's hand, and he squeezed, willing her not to freak out at the fight that might happen in front of them. Maddox wouldn't stand in the way, not when North's honor and Logan's protectiveness were in question. The two men would have to find a way to deal with each other at some point.

Hopefully, without the loss of blood.

The two men faced off wordlessly, each with fisted hands.

Parker stood up and walked toward them while Lexi tried to hold him back.

"Mom will be safe, Uncle Logan, you know it," the kid said, and Maddox was grateful.

"How do I know that, Parker?"

"Because your wolf says so, just like mine," he answered calmly. "And, North, Uncle Logan is all that Mom and I have, so give him a break, okay?"

The two men stared at each other for a moment more then relaxed, the tension easing as quickly as it had come.

That this eight-year-old boy could diffuse the tension so quickly surprised Maddox, but he didn't say anything. There was something more to Parker, and he'd find out, eventually, but his wolf told him there were more things to consider.

"So, we hunt," Maddox said finally, letting Ellie lean into him.

"We hunt," Logan agreed, sealing their mission.

Maddox had a feeling they weren't done with these three, not by far.

9

The light from the moon danced on Ellie's skin, and her wolf begged to come forth, ready to be set free. She'd never been on a hunt with the Centrals—not once in all her years of torment and growing. No, her past life had never been as communal as that. If Corbin and her father had gone on hunts, they had been hunting the weaker wolves who they wanted out of the Pack. It had been a brutal reminder that the Centrals were on their own and held to no law—even if they hid it from the other Packs so they wouldn't be taken out.

She held back a shudder and inhaled the crisp air, needing to calm down so she wouldn't alert the others with her fears. The twins thought they knew all, but they didn't know the barest brutality that lay beneath her skin like a stain that could never be washed away. Lexi already knew too much, even if Ellie wasn't sure what the other woman knew.

She let her mind wander to the hunts she'd been on with the Redwoods. She'd felt free, fearless, and strong—if only for a moment. Rather than hiding and shifting in her room so Corbin wouldn't find her, she'd hunted with wolves who actually loved and cared for one another.

Ellie had always been aware of the looks the others, the ones who had never trusted her, gave her, but she'd done her best to ignore them. The Jamensons had brought her into their fold, even if Maddox hadn't wanted her the way she so desperately wanted him.

They had made her family.

Then her brother had taken that away.

He was really the only person she could think of—other than Caym—who would kill her new Pack mates in order to frame her. She might have been able to stay and clean up the damage before, but not anymore. Too many people had died at the hands of her blood, and she'd begun to lose hope.

She'd find a way to clear her name. There was no way she'd lose everything she'd gained in such a short amount of time, even though she had no idea how to go about doing that.

The only way she could think was go to the Centrals directly to find their mole. The Jamensons were working on their end to find it, so Ellie would do her best to help on her end. Meaning she'd enter the hole of depravity where it's source had long since stalked her and try to not only find a way to make it right, but find a way to help the Redwoods for their future.

Ellie shuddered again, this time swallowing the bile that followed.

She *really* didn't want to go back, though there might not be a choice.

"Ellie? What's wrong?" Maddox asked as he came to her side. The wind brushed his hair from his face, the lack of hair showing the scar against his skin more than usual. Concern filled his gaze, and she pulled herself up so she wouldn't fall into his arms or grab him and keep him close so she could also protect him.

She wasn't a fully dominant wolf, nor was she a submissive one, and Maddox made her want to act like both.

"Just getting ready for the hunt." It wasn't exactly a lie, but she wasn't about to tell him what she'd been thinking about.

He already didn't want her, and she couldn't let him see exactly how ruined she was...how much she didn't deserve him.

God, she hated the way she sounded. She also didn't make any sense considering she was mad that he didn't want her either. Mating made her crazy, that had to be it. She needed to heal, to be free, but she didn't think that would happen any time soon, not with them being on the run.

"If you're sure." His hands fisted as if he had to hold himself back from reaching out to her.

Or, maybe that was just her own desires making her see things.

"Of course." She looked into the surrounding forest, and the shadows grew deeper, their spindly fingers almost reaching out for her. "I don't want to go for too long, just long enough to make sure my wolf is happy."

Well, as happy as she could be.

"I'm with you on that," he said, and he abruptly turned away from her. "Plus, I don't know that I like leaving North alone here."

"He'll be with Lexi," Ellie added, wanting to know what Maddox thought of that.

"Yes, that." He smiled slightly, and Ellie held back a sigh. She really needed to stop acting like a teenager. Or, at least how she assumed a normal teenager acted.

Back when she'd been a teen, she'd been different from everyone else.

Then she'd met Maddox, and everything had changed.

She hadn't known she was his mate yet. No, that wouldn't come until she reached adulthood, but she remembered the way he'd been chained to her brother's table. She remembered the way he'd screamed when Corbin had scarred him. She remembered how she'd done her best to help him, only to find herself on the receiving end of Corbin's pure rage for the first time.

Corbin had enjoyed toying with her since she'd been a

toddler, but it had been her betrayal that had led him to his new fascination.

She swallowed hard as she stripped down so she could change to her wolf, doing her best to not look at Maddox as he did the same. They both had scars, most of his from Corbin—the same as her. She didn't want to invade his privacy, and as wolves, they might be okay with nudity, but they wouldn't cross the line and comment on things better left hidden...at least for now.

The moon danced across her skin as she knelt on all fours, letting her wolf wash over her. Her bones broke and reformed, the muscles and tendons tearing then tying together. Her face elongated, and fur sprouted over her body. She wasn't as fast at transforming as North—not by far—but she was faster than she'd been when she'd been with the Centrals.

Apparently, even a fragile form of acceptance made her wolf stronger, calmer.

Finally, she stood on four paws by Maddox's side. She threw her head back and howled, relishing in the wolf, in the freedom, and in the future she could have.

It had to be better than what she'd had before.

It had to.

10

Over Sixty Years Ago.

Ellie watched the broken man make his way across the Central's border. She hoped he made it home, but she wasn't sure he'd do so. Corbin had hurt him badly, yet there was nothing she could do about it, other than try to get him free. She couldn't cross the wards, not when her own life was in danger.

She'd done the best she could. It would be up to the broken wolf to find his way home and heal. She just prayed to the goddess he would be all right.

She looked over her shoulder as she suppressed a shudder. There wasn't any more time for woolgathering and praying. She needed to make it back to her chamber before Corbin found out she'd escaped.

He hadn't chained her in her room—not like he'd done

with her twin and cousin—but Ellie knew it would be only a matter of time.

And if he found out she'd helped his prisoner...

She swallowed hard.

Best not to think about that.

Ellie crept along the edge of the woods and held her breath. She just needed to pass through the closest door, and she'd be okay.

She heard the growl before someone slammed her into the ground.

"You bitch!" Corbin yelled as he smashed his fist into her side.

She struggled beneath him, holding her tongue and trying not to scream... He loved it when they screamed. Her side ached, and she feared he'd broken something.

Goddess, don't let me die. Not yet.

The goddess didn't answer her, as usual, but still she prayed that she wouldn't die at her brother's hands.

"You let him go, you whore! Did you fuck him? Is that why you let him go? You're mine, Ellie, mine." He sneered the last word, and she swallowed hard, fear filling her as bile rose in her throat.

He growled at her silence and slapped her hard, her cheekbone shattering under his brute strength.

"I've been patient with you, waiting for you to grow enough to understand the way things work, but you've disappointed me, Ellie." An odd gleam entered his eyes, and Ellie wanted to take back her prayer to the goddess.

Maybe some things were worse than death.

He hit her broken cheek once more. Blinding pain assaulted her before she screamed out, and then she succumbed to the darkness.

Ellie woke much later, or at least it felt that way. She blinked away the darkness and tried not to cry. Her arms were chained above her head, her body hanging from the ceiling. Her toes barely brushed the floor—not enough for her to relieve the ache on her shoulders, just enough so she could hope for relief but never find it.

Her brother was always an expert in finding ways to torture those he wanted to feel the full pain of his wrath.

Ellie had never been on the receiving end though.

She'd been stripped to her undershirt and panties, so at least she wasn't naked like most of those who had been in this room. Her cheek ached, but she knew it was healing due to her wolf—meaning she'd been out of it for at least a day.

The side where Corbin had hit her before only hurt a little, so she'd healed a bit at least. The room was lit with only a bare bulb. The walls were dirty and sprayed with dried blood. Corbin liked to keep some rooms filled with the evidence of his torture, while others were clean to the point of madness. Each room had a specific purpose, and this one's was to taunt her with what was to come.

She knew she shouldn't have helped that man...but she hadn't been able to stop herself. Something had beckoned her to do it, and she'd succumbed.

Now, she would pay the price, but at least that man had a chance.

There had to be a good reason for it all...there had to be hope.

The lone door opened slowly, and Corbin strolled in, a frown on his face. Her brother looked just like her and the rest of her family, dark eyes, dark hair, tan skin, but where others looked normal, he looked like the depraved man he was.

"It's good you're up, sister mine," he said, his voice low. "I'm going to have fun with my new toy. I've waited for you to be by my side, and yet you've shunned me. Now, I will beat this new found strength out of you."

She blinked, her mind not really registering what was about to happen. How could it? Though she'd never been loved—not truly—she'd never been in this position before. For some reason, she'd always held on to the hope that Corbin might change...that he might show mercy.

Not anymore.

"If it's any consolation, I won't rape you," he drawled, and relief filled her. "I'm not that grotesque. Don't look that happy about it, dear sister. No, I have friends who will do that for me. They're waiting right outside the door in fact. We're going to take every ounce of dignity and fire in you and strip it away. You've lost the right to hope."

He smiled then, and a little part of her died.

No, no, this couldn't be happening.

She'd never even kissed a man before...goddess no.

The door opened again, and three men walked in behind Corbin.

She took a deep breath and screamed.

Her brother might have liked the anguish, but she wouldn't go down without a fight...even if it was hopeless.

The other men smiled, and she closed her eyes.

Maybe there wasn't a reason to hope at all.

11

Over Two Years Ago.

E llie watched as the demon killed her sister, drinking her blood. Fire raged within her, but she didn't say a word.

She couldn't.

Her sister and cousin had long since given in to their fates and had died inside. Their bodies had been the only things left keeping them going...

Now, they were gone.

Mixed with the fire was a strange and sad relief. At least they wouldn't be in pain anymore.

Unlike her.

She'd always been the one to mouth off though. Since that first time Corbin had locked her up in his dungeon, she'd grown a thicker skin, fighting back to protect those weaker and taking the beating and rapes so he left the others in peace.

It had all been for naught it seemed.

Slowly, she backed away from the crowd as they stood yelling for their new member. Some were scared she saw, but they hid it well. She knew that others had already left the Pack, hiding in areas far away so they wouldn't have to succumb to the evil that was sure to come with this new arrival.

Ellie made her way to her room, locking the door behind her. Though Corbin had a key and could get in anytime he wanted, it at least kept out the others...most days.

She'd tried to escape numerous times before, but Corbin and her father had always found her.

Her body shook at the reminders of what he'd done to her when she had been found. Corbin had kept to his word and had never raped her personally...but his numerous friends had taken their turns.

There didn't seem to be a point in fighting anymore, though she did. If it had looked like she'd given in, Corbin might have grown tired of her and killed her long before.

Even though there were worse things than death, she always held out hope that one day she'd be free to heal... free to just be.

She'd helped others escape and live... Maybe one day it would be her turn.

The sound of the click of the door being unlocked sent a quick prick of pain down her spine.

Corbin walked in, a smile on his face that scared her much more than a mere frown would.

"I see you're being as obstinate as ever, dear sister," Corbin said as he strolled toward her. Instinctively, she reached out to slap him, but he caught her wrist, his nostrils flaring. "Such impertinence. You'd have thought it would have been long beaten out of you. No matter, you're needed somewhere else now."

Ellie stood still, her pulse racing.

What on earth could he need from her?

"It's too bad about the others who died, but really, I was done with them anyway."

Hatred filled her at the callous mention of the family he'd killed—or had served up on a platter for the demon to kill.

"I wouldn't speak now, if I were you," Corbin warned. "You didn't do your duty earlier and sacrifice yourself for the greater good of the Pack, so, now, you'll do what is needed."

Her heart raced at the thought of what was going to happen.

No. Not again.

"Caym, may I present my sister. Your prize." Corbin turned to the demon as he strolled into the room.

Caym looked like a fallen angel, his sharp cheekbones and dark hair striking against his dead eyes.

He smiled, and Ellie sucked in a breath.

Evil.

That's the only word that came to mind.

"Now, what shall I do with you, dear wolf?" Caym whispered, and that last bit of hope faded away.

There really wasn't a reason to dream anymore.

Her nightmares were real.

And inescapable.

12

Present Day

A wolf whimpered beside her, and Ellie blinked, her body shaking on four legs as she stood in the forest, unaware of her surroundings.

Something completely idiotic considering they were in danger at all times.

She turned her head toward the whimper and saw Parker by her side, his little wolf body shaking with either excitement or fear—she didn't know which.

Ellie leaned down and rubbed her head on his, trying to assuage his fears—if that's what they were. He leaned into her and sniffed, inhaling her scent.

If she'd been human, she would have smiled at the pup.

Parker and those innocents like him were the reason

she'd made it out alive during her years of captivity. She just needed to remember that.

She looked up at Maddox and Logan, who stared at her with interest. She lowered her gaze, not wanting to intimidate or show the weakness in her eyes.

Maddox padded toward her and nudged her side, and she held back a whimper of her own. She gave a small yip and trotted off, trying to put her memories behind her. The others followed as they continued their hunt.

Maddox ran by her side, and she felt grateful. Even though she wanted—no, needed—to stand on her own, the fact he that was there, if only in a promise of hope, helped her carry on.

Her own darkness was rife with pain and memories she couldn't bear, but maybe one day, she'd be able to face her own fears...and past.

Maybe one day she'd be good enough for Maddox and for the Pack that had welcomed her—if only for a brief time.

Maybe one day...

13

E llie hugged the blanket around her shoulders tighter, suppressing a shudder. It might have been sunny out, but that didn't stop the cold from seeping into her bones. The darkness seemed to creep in, trying to suffocate her with its barrenness and shadow. She knew it was all in her head, but for some reason, she couldn't settle. Something seemed off—as though their calm was about to explode into a storm of hatred and death.

She wasn't a seer or anything of note, but she had a feeling that it didn't matter what she thought was real or not. The dangers were coming, and death was on its trail.

They'd been at the cabin for a full day now, and nothing had been decided past reserving their strength for when and if the Centrals found them. She knew Maddox had another plan up his sleeve—he always did—but she didn't know if it also contained their three new companions.

"Ellie?"

She turned at the sound of Parker's voice and smiled. He was such a quiet child that she normally didn't even hear him coming. That normally would have scared her, but for some reason, she felt a kindred spirit within this boy. He, too, had no home and no family but the ones who protected him now, even if it meant their own life.

She looked into those hazel eyes and held back a frown. There was something different about him, yet she couldn't put her finger on it. Maybe it had to do with his father since, though he looked like a miniature version of his Uncle Logan, he still had traces of someone else.

Ellie blinked and tried to clear her head before finally answering the boy. "Sorry, I was woolgathering. Is there something you need?"

Parker looked her in the eyes, and Ellie held her ground, refusing to lower her gaze and show her submission—an odd thing to have to do with a child. This one, however, seemed to be full of power he didn't know what to do with.

The boy finally shook his head. "Sorry to stare you down. I can't help it, you know? My wolf wants to make sure everyone knows that I'm not going to roll over for them, but then I feel like I'm gonna get in trouble."

"It's because you're an alpha, Parker," Maddox said from behind him.

Both she and Parker jumped, not having heard the Omega approach.

"An *alpha*?" Parker asked. "Whoa. That's big."

Maddox shook his head then led Parker into the room, gesturing for the boy to sit next to Ellie. She shuffled over, making more space, keeping her blanket tight around her because the cold had never left.

Parker sat next to her with Maddox sitting on the other side of him. Parker drew his knees up to his chest and looked so much like the young boy he was, not the alpha wolf that wanted to control him.

"You're an alpha, not *the* Alpha," Maddox said. "That means your wolf is very dominant, much like your Uncle Logan's."

"Does that mean I have to be in charge of a Pack?"

Parker looked so confused—so lost—that Ellie gave in and wrapped an arm around his shoulders, bringing him into the blanket with her. He stiffened for a moment before leaning into her. Her wolf nudged at her, needing to comfort the boy just as much as she did.

Maddox gave her a soft smile, and her wolf yipped in joy.

"No, Parker, not unless you find your own Pack or you become Alpha of an existing Pack. Both are nearly impossible to do anymore. The Packs are clearly defined, and most lone wolves don't want to form their own Pack and deal with all the politics, and the already formed Packs are led by families with the goddess' magic to lead them."

Ellie ran her hand up and down Parker's back as he relaxed at Maddox's words.

"Parker, you're dominant, an alpha. That means your

wolf is really, really strong. You're going to want to protect all those around you even if they don't want protection. It's going to feel like an irrational fear to you, but your wolf *needs* it. Also, any other dominant wolf around you is going to set your own wolf on edge. The difference between an alpha and a wolf who only wants to dominate is their own control."

Ellie felt Parker nod, and she squeezed his shoulders. This was Maddox in his element. Even though he wasn't using his magic or connection to the Pack, he was still calming the boy and explaining what it meant to be a wolf. She'd always known he was good at what he did, but she hadn't really seen it in action.

There had to be a way she could fit into that—a way she could help.

She didn't want to feel useless anymore.

"What you did just now to Ellie is natural. She's a stronger wolf than most, I've seen her fight and hunt, so your wolf wanted to make sure her wolf knew you were there, but your wolf also didn't know what to do because she's not as strong as she should be, right?"

Ellie froze. What the hell did he mean by that? Shouldn't they be having this conversation between them and not in front of an eight-year-old boy? Pain sliced through her. Was that why he didn't want her?

Was she not good enough?

Maddox gave her a sharp look, and she saw his words had finally dawned on him.

"Damn, Ellie, that's not what I meant."

She raised her chin but didn't say anything. He'd have to explain himself to her.

Parker let out a little growl and turned to block her from Maddox.

Maddox let out a sigh and shook his head. "I'm sorry, Ellie. I only meant that your wolf is hurting and dominant wolves want to help you, not that you're damaged."

Ellie flinched. She hated that word.

Hated it.

Even though the word might describe her perfectly, she didn't want the man she cared about to think of her that way.

Parker let out another growl, and Maddox reached out to cup her face. The boy shoved Maddox out of the way and snarled.

"Be nice. You don't get to touch her after what you just said."

Ellie's eyes widened at the display. Though what Maddox had said hurt, she knew he hadn't meant it that way. Or, at least her brain did—her heart was a whole other matter. Parker, on the other hand, didn't need to be in the middle of it.

"Parker, I'm fine. Maddox is just trying to explain why your wolf wants to protect me like you're doing, even though it sometimes want to growl and act surly like you did before."

"But he made you sad," Parker argued, but his body

relaxed, and she pulled him closer, letting his little body calm.

This was what it meant to be Pack—even if he wasn't technically hers. Her wolf wanted to comfort him as much as his wolf wanted to do the same.

"I think I made myself sad," she explained. "What Maddox said was true, though he and I will have to talk about exactly what it means privately, okay?" She was talking to Parker but gave Maddox a look when she said it. He nodded, and her wolf seemed to relinquish a bit of her annoyance.

The human in her, however, needed more than a nod.

"Okay," Parker mumbled. "It's hard being a wolf."

Her wolf reached out to him, calming his, and it took all her effort not to pull him closer into her arms and smother him. Apparently, her maternal instincts were showing themselves off in full force.

"I know, buddy," Maddox said. "Believe me, I know. It's got to be even harder without a Pack, though your mom and uncle are doing their best from what I can see."

Parker nodded.

"I bet they've also told you how to control your wolf, right?"

Parker nodded again, lowering his gaze.

"You're doing a great job for your age, Parker," Maddox explained. "You have a lot more to learn, but your mom and uncle know what they're doing. Listen to your wolf and use your control. It takes time to learn how to find a delicate balance, but I can tell you're well on your way."

"Do you think we could go home with you?" Parker asked, and Ellie's heart ached for him. "I want to be part of a Pack."

Maddox met her gaze, and Ellie wanted to pull them both into her arms and never let go.

"That's something we'd have to discuss with Lexi and Logan, Parker," Maddox answered.

Ellie couldn't tell what he thought would result from that conversation. On one hand, her wolf felt safe with these three strangers. On the other, she didn't speak for the Pack and didn't know what they'd do—especially with the state of things now.

Parker let out a sigh. "I guess that's a no."

Maddox reached out and gripped Parker's chin, forcing the boy's gaze to his. "That means we need to talk about it, Parker. I won't lie to you, and I won't promise you anything but an open mind from my end. Okay?"

"Okay. Sorry for freaking out on you."

Ellie ran her hand through his too-long hair. "You didn't freak out. You're just a growing boy who happens to also be a growing wolf."

Parker smiled, and Ellie blinked. There was just something about him that reminded her of someone, but she couldn't place it.

"Thanks. I'm going to go see what Mom and Uncle Logan are up to. Stay warm, okay? You looked like you were really cold when I came in." With that, Parker walked out of the room, leaving her alone on the couch with Maddox.

She shifted uncomfortably as she pulled the blanket around her tighter.

"Are you cold?" Maddox asked as he moved closer.

She could feel his body heat and resisted the urge to lean into him, if only for his warmth.

"I don't know why I can't warm up," she finally answered.

Maddox shifted again and pulled her into his arms. She froze for a moment before leaning into him, inhaling his crisp scent. She could feel his breath on her ear as he ran a hand down her side, warming her in more ways than one.

"This helping?" he asked, his voice gruff.

"Yes, but why are you holding me, Maddox? We need to talk."

Maddox let out a sigh and held her closer. "I know. I'm just trying to figure out what to say."

"You can start with how you don't want me." Her voice was stronger than she'd thought possible, but she still wasn't sure she wanted to hear what he had to say.

Maddox shook his head. "It's not that..."

Ellie's eyes widened. "Really? So this surly attitude and pushing me away is what...you saying you can't live without me?"

"Ellie..."

She opened her mouth to speak and froze as a wolf howled in the distance.

No, not in the distance...it was close.

"What was that?" she asked as they both stood quickly, the blanket falling to her feet.

"Not one of us," Maddox whispered and took her hand. She squeezed back, letting her wolf come to the surface, ready to fight if needed.

The rest of their group came into the room on alert, Lexi's arm around Parker.

"They've found us," Logan growled. "They hadn't come until you showed up."

"Logan, shut up," Lexi admonished. "They would have come here, eventually, anyway. We've been hiding for too long. It was bound to happen. Now, stop putting the blame on everyone else and help us figure out how we're going to protect ourselves."

Ellie wanted to hug this woman. Thank God there was at least one of them who could speak out when needed.

"We don't know who they are," Ellie said. They each gave her a look that made her want to shrivel up inside herself, but she held her chin high. "I'm just saying we don't know who yet, but we know it's probably the Centrals. What's the plan?"

"We fight," Logan said simply.

Maddox let out a growl. "We can't stay inside. All that does is let them surround us. We're going to go out and face them as men but shift if we have to." He leveled his gaze at Parker and Lexi. "Parker, I want you to shift too, okay? You're faster as a wolf. If anything happens to us, you run toward the Redwoods." He tore off part of his shirt and gave it to Parker. "Keep this with you. It has my scent on it, and my family won't hurt you because you're a pup and have part of me with you."

Parker nodded, his eyes wide.

"We don't have much time," North said as he rolled his shoulders. "Lexi, I assume you can fight in your human form?"

Lexi gave a wry smile. "Since it's the only form I know, sure."

Ellie nudged Maddox, and he faced her, worry on his face. "I can't shift as fast as the rest of you, and if we have to fight, I'd rather do it as a wolf."

She was strong as a wolf...more confident.

"We'll head out front," Logan said as he gave her a long look. Lexi, Parker, and North followed him, leaving Maddox alone with her.

He faced her and framed her face with his hands. Her breath caught in her throat as she looked up at him.

"We're going to settle this when we're done fighting everyone else," he whispered, his lips ever so close to hers but not touching. All she had to do was stand on her toes and she'd be able to kiss him...but she wouldn't do that.

He had to make the first move.

She'd always laid herself out for him, and she wasn't going to make herself look any more desperate than she already had.

"Change into your wolf, Ellie. I know you're stronger as

one, and I don't want you hurt." He lifted his gaze from her and looked behind her. "They're coming." He tucked a lock of hair behind her ear then moved away, giving her his back so she could shift.

She let out a shaky breath and stripped then knelt so she could shift. The change came faster since she was so worried, and when she was in her wolf form, she nudged the back of his legs.

He turned and gave her a strained smile. "You're a beautiful wolf. I hope you know that."

No one had ever told her that.

Her body warmed at his words, but she didn't move closer. The enemy was coming, and they didn't have time for this.

Maddox slid his hand through her fur for a bitter moment, as if he couldn't help himself, then turned toward the door. She followed, knowing this might be it.

Parker, in his wolf form, bounded to her and sniffed at her wolf before standing by her side. Lexi and Logan stood off to the side, Lexi holding what looked to be a bat, and Logan shirtless, ready to change if needed.

Maddox and North each took off their shirts, and Ellie had to hold herself back to keep from panting. So not the right time.

Parker nudged her leg, and she licked his head while his little body quivered in a mix of fear and excitement. She had a feeling this wasn't the boy's first fight, but, goddess, she didn't think he should have to deal with all of it.

Ellie could feel the other wolves surrounding them, their anger palpable. Maddox stood in front of her and gave her a nod.

"You run and take Parker with you if you can," he said so softly she wasn't even sure she'd heard him.

She lifted her lip to show fang. She wasn't weak—not anymore. There was no way she'd leave him. Parker growled beside her. Even with the little piece of cloth tied around his throat that made him look adorable.

Maddox growled. "I don't want you hurt. Please."

She didn't do anything, not that she could do much in her wolf form, but she wouldn't promise him something she knew she'd probably turn her back on.

Ellie could feel the other wolves moving closer, and her party stood on edge, ready to fight. They were on human territory, meaning there shouldn't be any fighting to begin with, but how the Centrals viewed things was another matter.

She inhaled their scents and held back a whimper.

There had to be over forty wolves around them.

And one was her brother.

Corbin.

"You're surrounded, Redwoods...and who is this...ah, Lexi and Logan, we meet again," Corbin crooned as he walked toward them, shirtless in the moonlight, his eyes glowing gold with his wolf right at the surface.

Logan froze then growled. It seemed the ex-Talons weren't the ones the Centrals were looking for at first.

"You're not welcome here," North drawled.

"This isn't your territory, and frankly, you stole my property, and I want it back."

Goddess, he sounded like a petulant child, not the Alpha of a werewolf Pack. Her father might have been evil and corrupt, but at least he'd had the backbone to be something more than whiny brat.

"She wasn't your property, and now she's a Redwood," Maddox said, his voice laced with anger.

"Really? She's a Redwood, is she? Not for long from what I hear."

No one said anything, and she was grateful. They'd left the den because the others needed to weed out the traitor. She and the twins were on their own...or at least they had been.

Corbin looked bored then snapped his fingers. The growls from the other wolves intensified, and they charged. All forty wolves—minus Corbin—came at them, their teeth bared, their souls black.

These wolves used to be her people, her Pack, and now, they were shallow husks of what they'd once been. The demon had taken their goodness—whatever miniscule amount some of them had—and had left behind nothing but tainted wolves intent on killing them.

She only hoped that the few wolves who had escaped the Pack before Caym had taken over were safe. Not every Central had been corrupt, but the ones that had been good had either been killed or had hidden in fear for their lives.

Lexi cracked her bat across the skull of a wolf as it came at her then moved on to another wolf. Logan growled and took out wolves, one by one, snapping their necks with his abundant strength.

Ellie had known he was a dominant wolf, but he was stronger than she'd thought.

North and Maddox took out the wolves on their other side, working silently as a team, killing each one swiftly.

A gray wolf came at her, and she moved in front of Parker. She sprang from her back legs and leapt on the wolf, digging her teeth into its neck. She worked her head back and forth, and the wolf beneath her whimpered, its body struggling against her. She bit down harder, severing its spinal cord before breaking its neck. She spat the blood out of her mouth and went at another wolf.

The enemy might have been greater in number, but most of the wolves were much weaker than them. The only reason the Centrals were winning the overall war was because of Caym—a fact that pissed them all off to no end.

Each of them took out more wolves, leaving bodies in their wake. She didn't move far from her spot, though, making sure Parker was covered. He might have been a dominant wolf, but he was still too small to fight.

Ellie saw a blur out of the corner of her eye and sucked in a breath as a wolf rammed into her side, knocking her to the ground. She wiggled from its hold, and it clawed at her, trying to rake its nails down her fur. Ellie turned from it and let out a yip before biting its neck, using all her strength to kill the wolf.

She lifted her head and let out a growl. When she'd moved to get out of the way of her attacker, she'd left Parker alone. Corbin shifted and his wolf ran toward the pup, his teeth bared.

Oh, God, she wouldn't make it in time.

Parker growled at Corbin, but it would be no use...he was just too small.

Corbin leapt at Parker, his teeth bared, but hit a moving blur instead.

An anguish-filled growl filled the air as North slammed into Corbin. Ellie threw her body over Parker's, but it was too late to save North.

Corbin slid fangs into North's chest, and blood began to pour from the doctor's body.

"North!" Maddox yelled, and he ran his body into Corbin's, dislodging the wolf from his brother's body.

Logan ran up to them and tried to claw at Corbin, but her brother merely ran back into the woods with his few limping wolves running behind him.

Oh, God.

No, this couldn't be happening.

They couldn't lose North.

14

Maddox placed his hands over North's chest, covering the wound as tears slid down his own cheeks. The blood pooled around him, seeping through his fingers as he tried to keep his brother's body together. Corbin's teeth had taken a good chunk of flesh with him, leaving a gaping hole that revealed muscle and bone. He was pretty sure something had pierced North's heart and maybe even his lungs.

Oh, hell, it was bad. It was real fucking bad.

If he'd been human, North would be dead. As it was, it didn't look good.

"Shit, Logan, get me something to cover his chest up," Maddox ordered, his voice shaky.

He looked over as Ellie lifted her body from Parker's and changed back into her human form. He could feel the magic wash over him as Parker did the same.

"North," she cried out as she went to his side, ignoring her nudity. "Oh, God, what do we do?"

North was their doctor, the one who could help in this. Maddox was just the Omega; he didn't know what the hell he was doing.

North tried to smile, but it came out as a grimace. "I need the Pack and Hannah. Just get the wound covered and get me back, and I'll be fine."

Maddox could see the hidden terror in his brother's eyes. He wasn't sure anyone else would have been able to. Hell, this couldn't be happening.

Lexi knelt by his side, tears running down her cheeks. "Thank you for saving my son."

"It was nothing," he said, his voice weak.

"Shh, don't speak. Save your energy," Lexi ordered.

Logan came running with a bag and a box of medical supplies. He threw the bag at Ellie, who caught it and started pulling out clothes for her and Parker while Logan knelt beside them, opening the box and taking out bandages as he did so.

"What do you need exactly?" the man asked, his voice just as gruff as Maddox's.

Hell, this wasn't good.

North reached up and tried to rifle through the box, and Maddox shook his head. "I know how to do basic first aid."

North's mouth hitched up in a smile. "Basic, eh?"

"Shush, you," Lexi said as she moved him ever so carefully so his head lay in her lap. Maddox watched as she carefully brushed his brother's hair from his eyes. "What did I say about talking? Save your strength." She looked up at Maddox, her eyes not full of fear but of determination. "What do we do?"

Maddox gave her a slight nod, his hands still holding his brother together like a patch-work quilt, then turned to Logan.

"Get the gauze pads and bandages. I'm going to try to pull him together so you guys can get him back to the Pack."

He didn't stop to gauge their reaction to his words but pushed harder on his brother's chest, trying to stall the blood flow.

"What?" Logan asked as he helped put the gauze and bandages on North's chest. The blood had slowed, but Maddox didn't know if that was a good thing since North had lost so much already.

"You're going to the Redwoods, asking for sanctuary, and getting my brother help."

"They'll kill us," Parker whispered though choked sobs.

Maddox looked up as a now clothed Ellie pulled Parker into her arms and kissed his temple.

"No, they won't," Maddox said as he and Logan bandaged up his brother. "You guys are going to drive there and make sure my brother lives. You are the enemy of the Centrals, and by that logic, we can only hope you aren't ours as well."

Logan growled, and Maddox shook his head.

"You guys were kicked out of the Talons for your own

reasons. My father might ask why, no, he *will* ask why, and you will tell him. You don't have to tell the rest of the Pack, but you *will* tell the Alpha. You'll be safer there, and you'll be saving my brother." He looked into Logan's eyes and thought he saw that spark of hope he needed to desperately cling to. "Please," he pleaded.

"Parker will be safe?" Lexi asked as she wiped North's brow.

"Yes," Maddox promised. His Pack would never hurt pups. "Please help my brother. We can't go back."

He didn't dare look at Ellie. He knew she'd be blaming herself when all of this wasn't her fault. No, that lay solely on her brother's shoulders.

"We'll help him," Lexi said while Logan growled.

"I'll go get the car," Logan said after a moment then stood. "We should be able to fit him in the back. Ellie, can you help Parker get some things packed so we can go?"

He ran off while Maddox looked at his brother, his twin, his lifeline. "You'll be fine."

North gave a weak smile. "Of course I will. You're taking care of me."

Maddox took a deep breath and tried to compose himself. "Damn straight I am. It's a habit of mine."

North laughed then blanched, pain arcing across his face. "Don't make me laugh."

Lexi cupped his cheek and smiled down on him. "Wimp. Now, stop moving so you can heal. We'll get you to your Hannah."

"Hannah's our Healer," Maddox explained, needing something to talk about other than what might happen to North.

"I assumed," Lexi said with a blush.

"She'll help him, and then everything will be okay," Maddox said, rambling now.

"Of course," Lexi said with a strained smile. "You...you can't leave us, okay, North? You saved my son, and I need to repay you."

"Not necessary," North whispered as he looked into her eyes.

Maddox felt as though he was intruding on something personal, but he couldn't leave them alone, not when his brother lay in pain, dying in his arms.

Maddox looked up as an SUV drove toward them and stopped. Logan jumped out and opened the back door.

"Okay, we're going to have to get him carefully," Logan explained. "This is gonna hurt."

"I'm ready," North croaked.

"I'll sit in back with him," Lexi said. "Just to make sure he doesn't jostle too much."

Maddox had a feeling it was more than that, but he wasn't going to argue, not when he was leaving his brother's life in strangers' hands.

He leaned down and kissed his brother's temple. "Stay safe, my twin. You'll be okay. Our Hannah is amazing at what she does."

"Keep Ellie safe, Maddox," North whispered. "Not just from the outside, but from the inside as well."

Maddox held back a retort, knowing what his brother said was not only true, but necessary.

"I'll keep her safe."

"Talk to her, explain why you're staying away. Then don't stay away. Life's too short, Maddox."

Maddox closed his eyes and shook his head. "Worry about yourself and your three new friends. I'll stay with Ellie."

"Be safe," North said, his voice weak.

"Always."

He and Logan carefully lifted North into the back seat, letting his head rest on Lexi's lap. Parker and Ellie came out of the house, carrying bags, and put them in the back. Ellie's face was pale, but she stood strong.

Parker came up to him and wrapped his arms around Maddox's waist. "I'll take care of him, Maddox. I promise."

Maddox swallowed hard and hugged him back. "I know you will. This wasn't your fault."

"I'll make sure he doesn't regret what he did," Parker vowed. He was a boy with too much knowledge of pain and darkness for his age.

Logan came up and pulled Parker away. "They might not welcome us with a bloody wolf in the back."

"I called them to warn them," Ellie said, surprising him.

"What?" Logan asked.

"I called Edward and told him what was going on. I'm still Pack, even if the world thinks I'm a killer."

"Ellie..." Maddox started, but she shook her head.

"We'll deal with my insecurities later. Get North to his family. They're waiting on him and won't cause you problems. Okay?"

Maddox blinked and cursed inwardly. He should have thought of calling his family, but he'd been so intent on taking care of North, all sense seemed to have left him.

He watched as the ex-Talons drove away, taking his brother and the only physical barrier between him and Ellie with them.

"He'll be okay," Ellie whispered as she slid her hand in his.

He held on tightly, needing her more than he wanted to admit.

"I know."

"What do we do now?"

Maddox blinked but didn't say anything. What else was there to say? The night had taken over, the enemy had tried to destroy them—almost succeeding—and now he was left alone with the one person he'd vowed never to be alone with.

He'd already given into his own impulses and pulled her into his arms earlier. God, had that been the same day? It felt as if it had been years ago, but in fact, less than an hour had passed since he'd pulled Ellie into his embrace and tried to warm her.

He shouldn't have done it before, but for the life of him, he couldn't fight it. He didn't *want* to fight it anymore.

He knew he wasn't good enough for her, and he'd only cause her heartache, but his wolf ached for her, and the man wasn't far behind.

"Maddox? If you aren't going to say anything, we should at least go inside and clean up."

He swallowed hard and looked down at their linked hands. His brother's blood covered them, drying in some areas, staining his skin beyond recognition. Ellie's hand was also stained, but from holding his hand, not from North.

That was the problem.

He'd stain her, force her to wear his mark and his burden.

Unlike the blood on their hands, his "gift" wouldn't wash away.

What right did he have to do that to the woman he was fated for?

"Yeah, we need to clean the blood off." He swallowed hard, thinking about how much had soaked into the ground beneath their feet and also into their clothes. Goddess, North had to be okay.

"We will. They'll take care of North, Maddox. You have to believe that."

He shook his head. "I don't know if I can. Not if I'm not there to see it for myself."

She winced but pulled him toward the house. "You can still go, Maddox. I can stay somewhere on my own. You don't need to stay by my side and protect me from the Pack's eyes. I don't even know if they believe I've been shunned anyway."

"Ellie, you know I didn't mean it that way."

"You're saying too many things you don't mean a certain way, Maddox. After you wash up, why don't you tell me what you do mean?" She turned and faced him, their hands still tangled. "We're past the looks and lies, Maddox. We're going to talk this out and figure out a way to move on together or apart. Either way, our wolves deserve more. *I* deserve more."

She left him then to go to the bathroom while he stood there dumbstruck.

She did deserve more, but how did he explain that and not break her heart?

He wasn't sure there was a way.

He went to the kitchen sink and took a deep breath. The slight pink of the sky startled him, and he shook his head. It was almost daybreak. They'd spent most of the night worried and making plans for how they'd all leave to find a safe place. Then Corbin had come and shattered that semblance of peace.

Maddox wasn't even sure there had been peace to begin with, but this uncertainty was even worse. He only hoped his family would risk calling him to tell him and Ellie about North. He knew they needed to keep contact to a minimum so the traitor within the Pack would think he'd left with Ellie because she'd been shunned.

There was only so much they could do outside the den walls though.

He hated not being able to help more, but there was nothing he could do, at least not yet and not until he and Ellie had spoken about the things they'd left unspoken for far too long.

He dried off his hands and walked into the living room where Ellie knelt on the floor, repacking her bag as if she wanted to be ready to go at a moment's notice.

"We need to talk, but first we need to plan," she said, not bothering to turn around. "Safety is more important than angst at the moment."

Ellie might have been shadowed and fearful of most who could harm her, but every once in a while, she'd get these sudden bursts of strength and attitude. He lived to see more of those, to relish in the fact that she was healing.

Even if it was without his help.

"I think we can stay here for a bit," he said as he sat down on the couch, placing his head in his hands. He needed to stop and think. So much had happened in such a little amount of time he couldn't put it all together.

"Won't they be coming for us?" she asked as she turned to him but didn't move closer.

He could still smell her spicy and sweet scent as it was, so he was glad she stayed away from him. He didn't know if he could control himself if she stood closer.

"Yes, and they know where we are, but honestly, we don't have anywhere else to hide on neutral ground. The

Centrals will find us, no matter where we go, but I'd rather fight them on land I know and have the ability to protect."

"So we'll stay here for a bit then?" Ellie finally moved and sat on the coffee table in front of him, their knees barely brushing.

He sucked in a breath at the slight touch but didn't move.

"I don't think Corbin will think that we'll stay here. Plus, he's hurting. Bastard should have been hurting more, but at least he's in a bit of a fix."

She brushed a lock of hair from his face. Her touch was so gentle, so hesitant, that Maddox resisted the urge to pull her close and never let go.

"North will be okay, Maddox."

"I want to believe you."

"Then do." Her hand trailed from his hair to cup his scarred cheek, and he leaned into her touch, not caring that she again touched him where no one else had.

"Ellie, this can't happen," he whispered, but even to his own ears, he didn't sound as though he meant it as strongly as he had before.

She didn't flinch or move her hand. "Tell me why, Maddox. Does your wolf not want me? No, that can't be true. My wolf knows your wolf wants us together, so it has to be the man. Do you not want me?"

He closed his eyes, unable to look into her dark ones and lie...but did he need to lie?

No, it was time to tell her why. Tell her why she couldn't

be his and that she should move on so she could be happy because if anyone deserved to be happy it was her.

"Ellie, God, I want you. You have no idea how much I want you," he said quickly.

Her eyes brightened then narrowed. "Then why don't you want to be my mate? Am I not good enough?"

He shook his head and cupped her face with his hands. "You are incredible, Ellie Reyes. You are the strongest person I know. You're the one who I could see my future with, the one I'd want by my side if it was possible. I love the way you smile when you find yourself in a place you feel you're allowed to be happy. I love the way that, even though the world seems to be against you, you still try to show them that you're better than they think. I love that, no matter what happened in your past, you're determined to make your future brighter. I love the way the wind hits your hair in just the right way that it frames your face and still blows behind you, making you look like a proud warrior."

Tears spilled down her cheeks, and he wiped them away with his thumbs, needing her to know how much he wanted her, how much she meant to him.

"Ellie, you're precious to me. You have to believe that."

"Then why...why, Maddox?"

"Because if we were to create the mating bond, I'd break that fragile peace you've woven for yourself. I'm like the blood on your hands, Ellie. I'll stain you, break down the barriers you made, and ruin you."

Fire lit her eyes, and she pulled away from his touch,

leaving him bereft.

"Seriously? You're saying that you want me like no other and say all those beautiful things, yet do nothing about it? Is this really the it's-not-you-it's me talk?"

He shook his head and took her hand in his. She pulled back, but he tightened his grip. "Ellie, it's not that. I'm the Omega; I can't mate."

She snorted. "No, you only think that."

"When was the last time you knew an Omega that had a mate?"

"So you're saying that Omegas shouldn't mate, even though fate has given us a chance? The other Omegas might have been idiots and pulled away to protect themselves, but I thought you were better than that. I thought that *we* were better than that."

"Ellie, you're not to blame. I don't want to hurt you."

"Too late for that, you ass. You're doing it by saying we can't be together when you're just too scared to."

"It's more than just you and me; it's all the powers of the Pack, baby."

"Don't you baby me, Maddox Jamenson. You're going to tell me exactly what you mean right now because I'm tired of watching you and not having the courage to do anything about it. You keep telling me that I'm strong, that I'm a warrior. Well, hell, I haven't felt that. I've *never* really felt that, not where I came from. Now, you're going to have to deal with this new me you seem to think I am. What do you think I can't handle as your mate? What am I too weak for?"

He let out a breath and pulled her to his lap, needing to hold her, despite what he needed to say. She struggled for a moment then relaxed.

"Just because I'm sitting on your lap doesn't mean I've given in. You have a lot to explain."

"I'm the Omega, Ellie. That means I can feel every emotion of every member—no matter what it is. My powers are even stronger than my dad's sometimes. Most days I'm so overwhelmed I feel numb and electrified at the same time. Sometimes I feel as though there's so much pressure on my chest my heart could burst at any moment. Those days I can't breathe or think, and I need to hide in my room so I can recover and try to act normal. That's all it is, Ellie— an act."

She cupped his face and leaned so her forehead touched his. "Oh, Maddox..."

"With the mating bond, you'd feel all of that, Ellie. And it wouldn't be like a normal Omega where you'd have years to get used to it. Instead, you'd get it all at once."

She shook her head. "It would be worth it."

"How can you say that? You don't know the pain."

"No, I don't. I do know you're the strongest man I know and that whatever you do you do with grace. Let me ease your burden, Maddox. Let me help you. Bay and Adam share their duties as the Enforcer mated pair, same with Jasper and Willow with the Beta's powers, and so do the rest of your family. You feel you can't do it all alone? Then let me help. Let it be *my* decision."

He ran his hand up and down her back, unsure of himself. "What if it doesn't work that way? What if it makes everything worse, and I lose you?"

"Then let it be my choice. I want to help. I want to be with you. Our wolves *need* each other. I know fate is cruel sometimes, but she doesn't give us more than we can bear... it only seems that way at our darkest moments."

"You'd choose me?"

He'd never thought of it as sharing a burden rather than sentencing her to pain.

What if they could do this?

If anyone was worth taking the chance with, it was Ellie.

"Of course, Maddox. We don't have to mate all the way. I know the mating urge is strong, but we can still take it slow. I'm just saying we need the option and opportunity. Let us get to know each other as people and wolves with a promise of a future instead of hiding from what could have been."

He moved her so she straddled him, his cock nestled against her heat, and they both gasped.

"Slow, Ellie. I need to know you've thought this through."

She smiled, tears filling her eyes, though she didn't cry. "I've already thought it through, but if it makes you feel better, we can take it slow."

He was done talking, done with words and all that they meant. He needed to taste her, to feel her in his arms.

He ran a hand through her hair, loving the soft feel in his hands. She leaned forward but didn't say anything, didn't breath. Maddox moved closer, letting his lips barely brush hers, the soft feel almost his undoing. He moved his head side to side so their lips gently touched each other's then pressed harder, loving the way she melted against him, her mouth parting ever so slightly.

He let his tongue barely trace her lips, teasing, testing, then opened her mouth farther, blending her moan with his own. He knew she needed softness, and he'd be the one to give it to her—even if it hurt to hold back.

Her mouth parted wider, and his tongue tangled with hers, their kiss deepening, their breath quickening. He pulled back, nibbling on her lips, moving his mouth along her chin to her ear. She turned her head to the side so he could nibble down her neck to the place where he'd mark her when they were ready.

He traced his lips back through his trail until he met her mouth, kissing her softly, wordlessly.

His wolf howled in pleasure, and he pulled back, cupping her face so he could look her in the eyes.

"Slowly," he whispered, his voice shaky.

"Slowly," she agreed, her lips partially swollen from his kisses.

Hell, slowly would kill him, but he needed to give her a chance to back out—something that would also kill him.

A promise meant nothing without the threat to break it up on its trail, and he wouldn't let her hurt for him. They'd find a way to make it work.

They had to.

15

A few days later, Maddox watched Ellie stretch in the living room, her body tight and yet soft in snug yoga pants and a light top. They'd just come back from a defensive run, setting traps around the cabin so they would be warned if another encroached on their territory. They'd also been training so Ellie would be more prepared to fight as a human. Yes, North had helped her when she'd lived in the den, but she still wasn't comfortable in her skin. Plus, the thought of his twin anywhere near Ellie still made Maddox want to rip the man to shreds.

Best not to think about that.

Self-confidence was one of the pivotal tools in fighting for one's life, and Ellie hadn't had any before she left the Centrals. She'd survived on what little—or nothing—she had until she'd found a way out with Reed and his mates, but it hadn't been easy. Then he'd broken her again because he'd shut her out. He was as much to blame as Corbin in some respects.

Now, he had to show her he was actually going to try and be who she needed him to be.

North wasn't standing in the way anymore.

Maddox just needed to make sure *he* wasn't the one standing in the way.

This wasn't an about-face decision. He'd been slowly breaking down and imagining what she'd feel like against him, what she'd look like round with his child...what she'd feel like in the throes of passion.

He'd been an idiot for far too long—acting like Adam and pushing her away like his brother had with Bay, and Ellie had suffered for it. Maddox didn't want to hurt her, and he knew his powers could do just that. Once he completed the mating, she'd be at the mercy of fate and what it would do to their bond.

What right did he have to harm her that way? To risk everything she'd built in this short time because he wanted her in his life?

He'd stayed away because he cared for her, and, now, he was closer than ever for the same reason.

For her sake, he only hoped he wasn't making a terrible mistake.

"Maddox?" Ellie walked toward him, her chest heaving as she caught her breath. "What are you looking at?"

He gave her a small grin, unable to help himself from smiling at her anymore. "You."

She blushed underneath that sexy-as-hell caramel-dipped skin and lowered her eyes. Unlike most of the other times, he didn't think she did it to show her wolf's submission but because she didn't want him to see the emotion in her eyes.

He already knew of course. Hence the reason why he'd broken and kissed her before, promising more than he wanted to give, yet everything he desired in his future.

"What's next in our plan?" she asked, still not looking at him.

He lifted her chin with his finger, her skin soft under his. "Anything you want, Ellie. We're allowed to take a break to breathe."

He looked into those dark eyes and barely resisted the urge to take her lips, her body, and anything else he could do to prove he was worthy of her, prove she was better than him as well.

"What about if they attack?" she asked, the fear she tried to hide still evident in her voice.

He took his other hand and ran it through her hair, slightly tugging on the ends, loving the way her eyes darkened when he did so. She might have been fearful of what was to come between them because of her past, but he knew that, beneath all that, she was someone who would fit against him perfectly, enjoying what he gave her.

"We're as prepared as we can be. The only way it would be different is if we were hold up in a cave living on the earth—something we can do if necessary. We're safe here, Ellie. As safe as we can be, anyway."

Ellie closed her eyes. "I wish there was something we could do to fight back. I hate sitting around waiting for them to attack us."

Maddox held back a growl at the helplessness in her voice for he too felt the same way.

"We've consulted witches' covens, as well as Hannah, and you know we can't use dark magic or we'll be infected like the Centrals are. Their souls are gone, Ellie. Only those who chose to break free, like you, are more than empty husks to be used by Caym. We've made our den as protected as possible, and soon we'll fight back on their land. We'll go on the offensive when the Centrals are at their weakest— when we find that. Soon."

She looked up at him and lifted a lip, baring fang. "Good. It's about time we went to them."

Goddess, how he loved when she said *them* and didn't include herself with the Centrals. They were on the right track.

He traced her jaw with his finger, loving the slight intake of her breath, and looked deeply into her eyes. "Tell me what you want, Ellie."

She swallowed hard but didn't lower her gaze. "You, but not just...you know." She blushed then, and he held back a chuckle. That wouldn't be the best thing to do at the moment, not when she was so unsure of herself.

"Tell me what you want." She needed to be the one who

led, not him. He couldn't push her, even though she'd been the one who'd broken through his shields.

"I...I want to know more about you. I want to know everything, Maddox. Then...then we'll see." She gave him a coy smile that he wasn't sure was meant to be so but made her sexy as hell.

Then her words registered, and he blinked. She wanted to know him? Hell, baring his soul would be harder than baring his body, but he knew he'd have to do it. She was his mate, his life—or at least she would be if they let it happen.

"Okay," he said slowly.

Her face shuttered, she tried to take a step back. He gripped her waist, hating the way her eyes widened in fear before she tried to mask it.

Hell, her brother had done a number on her. Maddox couldn't wait to tear the bastard limb from limb.

Slowly.

"Ellie, don't fear me," he begged.

"I don't, Maddox, I swear. You just caught me off guard. I know you'd never hurt me."

That was a lie really, since he'd done just that by pushing her away for so long, but he'd find a way to fix it.

"I'll tell you anything you need to know. Just ask." He'd get over himself and share with her. He'd never done it with his family, but his wolf needed Ellie's—just as much as the man needed his mate.

"I don't know where to start," she said as she gave a

small laugh. "I have so many questions, yet I feel like I know you as much as your family."

Maddox shook his head. "They don't know everything, Ellie. You know as well as I do that I don't talk about much."

"True, which is why they're always so cautious around you—the same as me." She gave a self-deprecating smile, and he tugged her to the couch, pulling her to his side as they sank into the cushion.

He tried to think of something to start with, something to show he was trying. The only thing that came to mind that could prove he was trying, that he wanted to make this work, was telling her about his scar.

Hell, could he share that part of himself?

No one knew the truth, yet he *needed* Ellie to know.

"Over fifty years ago, your brother took me to his den because he thought I was North," he began, unable to look at her. He'd just proven that he had a weakness—he'd been captured. How the hell had this been a good idea? His wolf needed to show he was strong, not someone who could be captured so easily.

"That's why he did it?" she gasped, and Maddox froze.

"You...you know?" He froze to look into her eyes and saw not only horror but understanding. "It was you," he breathed. "You were the girl who saved me."

She gave a wobbly smile, and he leaned to take her lips, needing to remind himself she was real. She'd been his savior for so long, and she was *here* and his.

"I'd thought they'd killed you, Ellie. Oh, God, baby." He

kissed her again, her lips opening for him so he could taste that sweetness that was only her.

She pulled back and traced his scar. He swallowed hard but let her—again. Only Finn had touched it before Ellie had in recent times, and he couldn't believe he'd let it happen. Though the nerve endings were mostly dead at this point, and the scar tissue was so thick that it made it hard to smile or move his cheek, he could still feel her warmth, her softness.

"It was me. I was a teen then, but I remember you. I didn't know Corbin had thought you were North though. He never did tell me anything. I'm so sorry you went through that, my Maddox."

Her Maddox. He liked the sound of that.

"I'd heard a scream. I thought... you'd died."

Her eyes shadowed, and she nodded. "He wasn't happy I let you free."

"Oh, baby, you risked everything for a man you didn't even know." He crushed her to his chest, needing to feel her heart beat against his. He felt the wetness on his shirt as her tears slid down her face. "I'm so, so sorry he hurt you for helping me."

She wrapped her arms around his waist and squeezed. "I survived. As did you. You can't blame yourself for what Corbin did."

He pulled her from his chest so he could meet her gaze. "You can't blame yourself either. Nothing Corbin did was your fault." He didn't know the extent of what had happened to her, and he knew she wasn't ready to tell him —but she would.

"I'm trying," she whispered.

"God, we're a mess," he said, trying to lighten the mood.

"True, I guess that's what makes us mates."

She smiled at him, and he took her lips again. She tasted of berries and that sweet spice that was just Ellie.

"I don't want to hurt you, Ellie."

"I don't care, Maddox. We'll get through it."

"There's something you should know. I can't sense your emotions, and even though I'd love to know what you're feeling, I'm glad I can't."

Her eyes widened. "I had thought that, but I wasn't sure. You mean I'm cut off from you?"

"You're the quiet in my storm, Ellie Reyes."

She smiled. "I like that. I know it's too much for you with everyone around you. I like that you can relax around me. Well, you know, if you'd ever relax around me."

He laughed with her and kissed her brow. It was if the dam had broken and he couldn't get enough of her or her taste. This wasn't the way he usually acted, and he liked it.

"I'm trying."

"You don't have to try alone, you know. You don't have to do everything by yourself. I'm here now. We can take it one step at a time, but you're only hurting yourself—and me—if you pull away." She swallowed hard. "And I'd do the same if I pulled away as well."

He let out a breath then swallowed back tears. "We

might both be broken, but I think we can piece ourselves together."

"We don't have to be whole apart," she agreed. "That's what being a mate is for—to find those missing pieces."

He framed her face and looked down on her. "I want you, Ellie."

Her breath stuttered, and she nodded. "I want you too, but... I don't...I've never been with anyone other than when it wasn't my choice." She blushed and turned away, but he didn't let her.

Maddox held back a growl, determined not to scare her. He would kill any man who had touched her in her past and make them pay. Ellie was his to cherish, and anyone who had wronged her had forfeited their life.

He didn't know all that had happened to her, but he knew it had been bad. She wasn't ready to tell him, and he was okay with that. She'd tell him, eventually, and they'd heal together. He might not be able to use his magic to help her, but he could use his words, his actions.

"I'll show you what it means to make love, Ellie Reyes. I'll show you what it means to be with someone, to feel their every movement, their heartbeat, their life. I've never mated with anyone before. This will be a first for both of us, okay?"

She blinked but didn't say anything.

"It's just you and me, nothing from our past or present to harm us," he stressed.

She nodded. "I trust you, Maddox."

He sighed in relief at her words. "And I'll do everything in my power to earn that trust."

"You already have."

He tucked a lock of hair behind her ear. "Not yet, Ellie mine, but soon."

She let out a shaky breath and tried to smile. "So..."

He chuckled. "So indeed." Hell, he needed to just say it and get them past this wall they'd built up in order to protect themselves. "We're safe here, in this cabin, as much as we can be. I know we want to take it slow, and I think we are. Gods, woman, I want you so much I can barely breathe."

Her eyes darkened, and she smiled. "I want you too, though I think we've already covered this."

He laughed. "In a minute, I'm going to take you to the bedroom and show you exactly what it means to be touched by someone who cares for you in every way possible, but I need to warn you that I'm not going to mate you. Not fully."

She jerked back as if he'd slapped her and scrambled off the couch. "What?"

He cursed himself and stood, reaching out to her. "No, that's not what I meant. We're going to mate, Ellie, but I don't want to mark you, not yet." He pressed his finger to her lips so she wouldn't argue. "That will come, I promise. Our wolves will mate when we mark each other, but not yet. I want to ease us into this so my powers don't overwhelm you. I don't want to hurt you, so we're going to do as we talked about and take it slow."

"And I have no say in this?" She narrowed her eyes, and he ran his hands down her arms.

"I don't want to hurt you or your wolf, so we *have* to take it slow, Ellie. Please."

At the word please, her face softened. "If that's what you think you need to feel better about all of this, fine, but I don't think it will be an issue. You wouldn't have a mate in me to begin with if I couldn't handle it."

He nodded, not really believing her words. He was already risking her future, *their* future, by giving into temptation and heeding his wolf's desires. He couldn't let her suffer for him. Fate had been cruel enough to him and his family, and he didn't know what lay in store for them.

Maddox framed her face with his hands before lowering his lips to hers. "You are so beautiful, Ellie mine. I knew it the first time I saw you in the back of the SUV when Reed brought you back to our den. I might have acted like I didn't, but it was because my wolf wanted to attack anything that could have hurt you. I'm never going to let that happen again—me running and you getting hurt. I'm here, Ellie mine. I'm yours."

She stretched up on her toes and kissed him softly, her tongue hesitantly darting out to reach his. Though he desperately wanted to shred her clothing from her body and take her where they stood, marking her as his and showing her what it meant to be with someone who wasn't cruel, he knew he needed to take it slow.

He pulled back, leaving them both panting. "Sweet Ellie,

sweet, sweet Ellie." She blushed under that caramel skin of hers, and he led her to one of the cabin's bedrooms. They'd been sleeping separately and in shifts, but tonight, they'd be in one bed.

Maddox could practically taste the nervousness coming from her, and if he were honest, he was just as nervous. He wanted to make it good for her, yet he didn't want to scare her and go too fast, too hard.

"Tell me what to do," she whispered.

"Just be yourself, Ellie. That's all I'll ever ask of you. Well, that and tell me if something feels good, okay?" He quirked his mouth in a smile to ease her, and she gave a small laugh.

"Kissing felt pretty good," she said quickly as if she were embarrassed to have said it.

He lifted her chin and looked into her eyes. "Good, because there's more of that to come. We're going to go slow, Ellie mine. Slow and sweet. If I do anything that scares you, let me know."

She nodded. "Are...are you sure you can go slow?" Her eyes darted to below his waist, and he held back a chuckle.

He knew she saw his jeans strain at the hold his dick on him, but there was no way he'd go fast and hard—not this time.

"Don't you worry about him," he joked.

"He looks like he needs to be let out." Her eyes widened at her words, and he threw his head back and laughed.

"Well, I'm sure that'll happen soon."

"What I meant before was that I know we're wolves and that mates like to go...you know...hard. So if that's what we need to do the first time, we can."

Oh, his sweet Ellie. Gods, she hurt him just be revealing hints of what she'd gone through. His brave Ellie.

He ran his hands down her bare arms again before gripping her hips, and then he pulled her to him, her soft body flush against his hard one. His jean-clad erection brushed her belly, and her breath quickened.

"We'll go fast and hard next time. I promise you'll like it." Gods, he knew he would. "This time though is going to be different."

"Can we stop talking about it now?"

He chuckled and nodded. "Anything you say, Ellie mine."

16

M addox brought his lips to hers, this time deepening the kiss right away, letting their tongues tangle as Ellie rocked against him as if she couldn't help herself.

His wolf howled in triumph and nudged at him, wanting him to mount her right away.

Done with words, he slowly ran his hands up and down her body as he continued to kiss her lips, her jaw, her neck. She moaned and writhed against him, turning him on more than he thought possible. He pulled back and met her gaze, and he took off her top, leaving her full breasts bare. They were ripe—at least a handful—and were tipped with dark nipples that hardened in the cool air of the room...or under his gaze.

Either way, he groaned at the sight of them, though he also saw the scars that marred her sides and belly, He ignored them for now, needing her to know he saw her as a woman first and foremost—never a victim.

She raised her chin as if daring him to say anything about it, so he kissed her lips then trailed kisses down her shoulders to the valley between her breasts. He could feel her heartbeat quicken under his tongue, and he smiled before turning his attention to her nipples. He rolled one in his fingers while suckling on the other, gently biting down so he could gauge her reaction.

"Maddox..." she breathed.

Good.

He sucked and nibbled her breasts, alternating between the two while palming the other in his hand to show them equal, exquisite attention. Her breathing labored as he ran his tongue under each breast and then lower. He dipped his tongue in her belly button, causing her to jump. Maddox palmed her ass, keeping her in place, and looked up, running his tongue along the waistband of her pants where it met her skin.

"What...what are you doing?"

He smiled and gently pushed her toward the bed. The back of her legs hit it, and she froze.

"I'm going to taste every inch of you, and then I'm going to love you until neither of us can breathe. We'll both be so spent we'll just lie in a heap until morning, and then I'll take you again just because I can. Does that sound like a plan?"

Her eyes widened, and then she smiled. "I think I'm going to like being your mate."

He bit her hip slightly then laved at the mark to lessen the sting. Ellie gasped, so he bit her other side, loving the way she responded.

She looked like a goddess, standing above him topless, her hair framing her face and running down her back. A long lock fell over her shoulder, brushing her breast, and he twirled it around his finger, gently touching her nipple as he did so. He let the lock fall so it cascaded along her breast again and smiled.

He was going to love taking his time with her.

This was the only form of torture she'd ever go through again.

No, he couldn't think about that, not now.

Maddox felt her fingers along his brow, and he looked up at her.

"No dark thoughts, my Omega. Only good ones. Only us."

He kissed her belly then pulled back to nod. "Only us."

He wrapped the top of her yoga pants around his hands and pulled down, his gaze never leaving hers. She lifted one leg then the other as he removed them completely. He finally looked down and sucked in a breath.

"No panties?"

"They're in the wash," she whispered. "We don't have that many clothes, you know." She seemed almost embarrassed at the fact she was naked before him.

He'd have to do something about that—tell her how beautiful she was and how much he wanted her...even when he'd denied it for so long.

"I'm not complaining. Dear goddess, I'm not complaining."

Maddox held himself still, trying to gain control. Goddess, his Ellie was the hottest thing he'd ever seen. She had curves, yes, but they were made from strength and learning to be herself. Her hips flared out, perfect for his hold. He could imagine himself gripping her hard as he pumped in and out of her, either from behind or from above where he could look into those dark eyes of hers and fall so deep.

Ellie held a hand out then froze, as if unsure of herself.

"Ellie mine, what do you want? What do you need?" He trailed his fingers down her hips as he spoke, her soft skin tantalizing.

"I...I don't know." She shook her head, even as he felt her tremble beneath his touch. "I'm not good at this sort of thing."

He pushed back the anger at that statement. Not toward her, of course, but against those who'd taken away her innocence and the fragile hold on who she could have become. He'd find a way to make it up to her.

Starting right now.

He slowly sat her down on the bed, and then he knelt between her thighs. He then lifted her chin to meet her gaze directly.

"I already told you that you just have to do what feels good, my Ellie." He took her lips then, relishing her taste.

He pulled back and took off his shirt, loving the way her eyes widened while looking at his chest. He knew she'd risked peeks at him before in stolen glances—as he'd done to her even when he'd denied himself.

He kissed her again then trailed his lips and hands along her neck and shoulders. He felt her fingers delectably dance along his skin, and he smiled.

She was doing something she desired for once.

Good.

He lowered his head to her breast and suckled on the sweet berry, flicking his tongue as she panted against him. He shifted attention to her other breast, and she moaned, slightly rocking toward him. Again, like before, he licked and kissed down her belly until he reached her hips then pushed her back so she lay flat on the bed, her legs dangling off the end.

She was bare to him, only a small amount of dark hair on her mound drawing his attention to the glorious sight before him. To him, she was untouched, clean and fresh as a new day's snow.

Ellie leaned up on her elbows and stared down at him, so he met her gaze and lowered his face, letting his tongue press against the hood of her clit.

She gasped, her body freezing, but he didn't hold her down to kiss her more intimately. No, he'd never hold her down.

"Does that feel good?" he asked as he blew against her opening.

She shuddered then nodded, as if hesitant to say anything aloud.

"Good, my sweet Ellie. I'm going to taste you then make you come." He usually wasn't so vocal during sex, but this was different; this was Ellie. He wanted to make sure she knew everything that was to come, and frankly, this wasn't just sex...this was making love.

"You...you don't have to be so cautious with me," she whispered. "I'm not technically a virgin."

He shook his head then placed a kiss on both of her inner thighs. "This is your first time, darling. *Our* first time. This is just us."

She nodded, and then he leaned in to trail his tongue along her lower lips. He parted her before licking and sucking, savoring her sweet taste.

Ellie buckled off the bed, but again, he didn't hold her down. Instead, he kissed and rolled his tongue along her pussy and clit while trailing one hand along her hip, relaxing her at the same time.

Slowly, he circled one finger around her clit then lower to her core before entering her. Her inner walls clamped around his finger, and he smiled before licking her again. He worked in and out of her channel then added a second finger, curling them to find that special point that would take her over the edge.

"Oh...Maddox," she whispered, her voice a plea.

He sucked on her clit as he rubbed circles on her G-spot, growling softly as he did so, sending vibrations through his soon-to-be-mate's body.

Her walls clamped down on him tighter, and she screamed, coming in a glorious blush. He didn't relent, wanting her to come down slowly and still in the midst of pleasure.

Finally, he pulled away and stood above her.

Goddess, she was magnificent.

Her tanned skin had a rosy hue, her body slightly glowing from exertion.

He smiled at her, and she did the same.

"That...that was amazing," she whispered.

He'd known she'd never orgasmed before, and now that she had...goddess, he couldn't wait to make her do it again.

"You're the one who's amazing," he said as he slowly undid his jeans then let them fall to the floor.

Her gaze went directly to his groin, and he smiled.

"I see I'm not the only one caught on laundry day," she said wryly.

He chuckled and shook his head. "It would seem that way."

Maddox lowered his body over her but didn't touch her. He merely rested above her, with his forearms bracketing her head.

"Scoot up, darling, and rest your head on the pillow," he ordered softly.

Her eyes widened, but she did as he asked, her breasts

rubbing along his body as she did so. He finally gave in to temptation and kissed every inch of skin he could as she moved beneath him.

Ellie's hair framed her head, splaying on the pillow. Again, a long tendril fell down her chest, circling her breast. He was pretty sure that was his favorite lock of hair.

"Are you ready, Ellie mine?"

Though his cock strained, he didn't move, not wanting to scare her.

"Always, Maddox. Always for you."

She didn't duck her head at her words this time, and he let out a breath.

Progress.

He gently took her mouth, letting her juices on his tongue meld with the sweet taste of her mouth. She moaned against him, arching her back as she did so.

The act forced his cock to brush against her pussy, and he groaned.

Dear sweet heaven, her core was so heated he could barely breathe.

He pulled away slightly and gathered her arms one a time and pulled them above her head, tangling his fingers with hers so they held hands. He focused his gaze on hers as he positioned himself at her entrance and slowly, oh so slowly, entered her.

She was the sweetest torture known to man, and he'd gladly die right there, knowing he'd found his heaven.

There would be more times for hard and fast, but now it was all about the exploration...the moment.

Her breath quickened as he pushed deeper until he was fully seated, his cock buried within her sweet heat, his balls tight in anticipation.

"Ellie mine," he whispered then pulled back, her walls clinging to him.

He thrust back in then pulled out again, over and over until they found a rhythm that forced him to hold onto control. His wolf howled, knowing that this was true peace, true everything.

Their hands remained together, their gazes never wavering as he slowly thrust in and out until he watched the blush rise in her cheeks and her eyes darken, the rim of gold from her wolf glowing.

He howled as they came together, his seed filling her, cementing the first part of their mating. His fangs elongated, longing to finish the second part of the mating, but he held back, keeping his promise.

His heart shuddered as he felt Ellie's soul wrap around his, their mating forming in the most fragile of senses. Yet, he could feel it was a strong bond, one made from their pasts and their future...one that would not be easily broken.

Maddox leaned down and took her lips, feeling his own tears on his cheeks as Ellie cried as well.

Why had he taken so long to do this?

He'd been missing...everything.

Goddess, he'd been a fool.

He slowly rocked within her core, the small spasms still shuddering around him as well as along his spine.

They'd started the first of their mating, and goddess, it was more than he'd expected.

He only hoped it wouldn't be her downfall.

17

The sun slid through the blinds, and Ellie snuggled deeper into the bed, not wanting to break the fragile peace she held on to so desperately. The room smelled of warmth, sex, and a mating bond that she hadn't known would be so tactile...so full of life. A heavy arm wrapped around her waist, and she smiled. Her new mate wrapped around her, closer and more heated than a blanket. He smelled of warmth, wolf, and forest—only a bare hint of that brokenness that used to cloud him and his smile.

She could feel Maddox inside her heart, her skin, and her soul. Their bond flared, and the human halves of them entwined, settling into a newness that she wanted to explore.

This is what she'd been missing—what she'd needed.

They were finally mates in all ways that mattered—other than the marking. Their kind needed two forms of mating in order to remain fully together. The human halves needed to make love, Maddox's seed cementing that bond as he filled her in the most romantic and erotic of ways.

Soon, when they both were ready, they'd each bite down into the flesh part of the shoulders where it met the necks and mark each other. Their wolves would then be mates just like their humans. The physical reminder would fade over time, letting them have the opportunity to mark again and again, feeding their bond and enjoying the sensual side effects, but the bond would never fade. As time moved on, their bond would strengthen and grow new layers, forming into a relationship that was unique to them.

She understood his reservations on that accord though and would gladly wait for her wolf's mating to assuage both of their fears. He wanted to ensure his own pain wouldn't seep into her. He was afraid that she'd break under the stress of what his position in the Pack entailed. For some reason, she wasn't scared of it. The goddess had taken everything in her life, or at least had allowed it to be taken through Corbin, yet she trusted fate and all that came with it to ensure the bond would be strong enough for both her and Maddox.

It didn't make any sense, yet she couldn't find the power to fear their mating.

Ellie could feel his steady breathing behind her and knew he had to be asleep. Good, he hadn't been sleeping recently, at least not enough. His stress over North and her safety had stressed him to the point that she could see the faint lines around his eyes deepen with each breath when he was awake. She knew the demands of being the Omega weighed heavily on him, and now she hoped that she could ease that burden.

If he let her.

Well, to hell with that, she'd make him. They were mates, and he'd just have to deal with the fact that she wanted to be part of his life.

Maddox had brought her fire back—something she'd thought she'd lost long ago. She'd be damned if she lost it again.

She closed her eyes again and sank deeper into his arms. The world around them was falling apart, but for the moment, all she wanted to do was lie in his hold and forget her problems. It might sound selfish, but she'd never had that place to do so before. She'd never had that safe place.

Maddox was her safe place.

She felt a gentle brush of lips along her shoulder, and she moaned. Ellie moved closer toward him and smiled as his cock pressed along her backside.

"Good morning," he grumbled.

"Not a morning person, are you?" she teased and wiggled again.

He gripped her hip but didn't hold her still. No, like the night before, he let her set the pace and where she wanted to be. Goddess, she felt safe with him.

She wouldn't regret that decision.

He bit her shoulder gently, and she held herself still.

Her wolf clawed at her, wanting that mark that neither she nor Maddox was ready for. He kissed her where he'd nibbled and ran a hand up to cup her breast.

"No, I don't like getting out of bed, especially now that I have a delectable, warm woman next to me."

She smiled and turned in his arms. They'd made love three times the night before, and she was delightfully sore, but if he so desired, she'd take him with wild abandon.

It was odd how quickly things changed yet stayed the same.

Her mate smiled, the curve of his lip slightly tugging at his scar. Though others would have been afraid of the mark upon his face, it only showed her how much he'd endured —how much he'd survived. She wouldn't have taken the unscarred North, even if he'd been her mate. There had always been a choice. Maddox was for her.

Maddox brushed her hair from her face and kissed her gently. "I'd wake us both up in a manner that would make you blush, but I think you're too sore for that." He nibbled on her lip, and she sighed.

"I'm sorry," she whispered.

"Never be sorry for anything we do here." He kissed her again and pulled back. "I like you all rumpled, by the way."

She laughed softly and shook her head. "You're pretty rumpled yourself." She ran her hands through his too-long dark blonde hair. "You need a haircut though."

He raised a brow and scoffed. "I see how it is. One day as my mate and you're already trying to clean me up."

He said it in a teasing manner, so she didn't feel chastened. Instead, she loved the way he didn't treat her with kid gloves, even if he'd treated her softly the night before. There was a difference in trying to heal and trying to box her away never to be heard from again. She was just happy Maddox seemed to know the difference.

Maddox kissed her again then softly smacked her bottom. "Now, let's get cleaned up and started on the day. I want to do another patrol before we discuss our next plan."

She nodded, hating the fact that their small interlude would be over. Their realities were catching up with them, and they'd have to find a way to not only clear her name but protect their Pack as well.

They quickly showered together, Maddox being ever so careful with her soreness, ate a quick breakfast, and threw on their coats and everything else for a patrol of the area. The sun lightly warmed their skin, even as the cool wind bit.

She couldn't scent another wolf around them, only the vague remnants of the battle that had left North in pain and had forced the ex-Talons to leave and find sanctuary with the Redwoods.

Cailin had called to tell them that North was in their care, but that had been it. No other communication had been initiated to rest their fears. They could only pray that he'd be okay while she and Maddox hid away.

Damn it, she didn't want to hide. Not anymore.

There had to be something she could do to fix this.

There had to be a way she could contribute to the Pack's safety and eliminate her brother's hold over her for good.

Maddox tugged at her hand, and she glanced at him. She had far more to lose now, yet far more to gain and hold on to. She wouldn't stand by and let them take it away from her.

"Ready to head back?" Maddox asked as he looked away, his senses as alert as her own.

"Yes, then we need to decide what to do," she whispered, aware she was giving orders, where before she'd have been the one to either follow them or hide.

He nodded, and they made their way back to the cabin, tension crawling over her back and settling in her belly. They sat in the living room, facing each other on the couch as she tried to calm herself.

"We need to go to the Central's den," she blurted.

Maddox closed his eyes and nodded. "I know. We've always let them come at us, and that's only proven we've been weak."

She shook her head and took his hand. "No, you haven't been weak. You've made decisions to ensure the stability and sanctity of your Pack. While the Centrals were dark and used magic to let themselves become corrupt and evil, you've stood tall and lived in the white and gray. Your souls aren't tainted to the point of loss."

He cupped her cheek, and she leaned into his palm. "Yet we've lost so many because we can't go dark, because we don't want to risk others just so we can win quickly."

"At least you've fought, Maddox. What have I done?"

He growled softly, and she froze. "Never think that about yourself. You stood up for yourself for years."

"No, I let Corbin reign over me." Her voice shook, but she didn't back down—not anymore.

"You lived, Ellie mine."

"And for what? I lost my family—the ones that could love—because I couldn't fight back." Tears fell down her cheeks, but she didn't brush them away.

He kissed her cheeks, licking up her tears before pulling away. "You did fight back, Ellie. Don't you see? He kept you alive because of the fire in here." He pressed his palm between her breasts over her heart. "You're stronger than you think, baby. You fought to protect me when I was at my weakest. You saved me, and you saved Josh, Reed, and Hannah. You got all of us out of the den and protected them, even though you knew you'd probably die in the process."

She tried to pull away from his hold, that familiar shame unable to be washed away so easily. "Josh still turned into a partial demon, and your Pack was still hurt from it."

He pulled her to his chest, and she let him run a hand through her hair. "You saved them, Ellie mine. You fought to protect those who needed it. You're stronger than you think," he repeated. "You've been strong all along. It's not the strength of what you could have done, but the strength of your past actions that prove you deserve something far greater than what you've got."

"Maddox..."

He kissed her softly, shutting her up quite nicely.

"I know you don't see it, but you're one to look up to, baby girl. My family already does as do countless others in the Pack—the ones who see past the hurt and stigma of who you were forced to live with for so long. You've got the heart of those who protect others, and I'm never going to let you forget that for as long as I live."

She looked at him as if she'd never seen him before. It made no sense. She'd always thought she'd been weak to allow Corbin to control her for so long, but maybe she'd been wrong. Maybe her rebelling and trying to free others had been something more than just guilt.

Ellie took a deep breath and wrung her hands. "I don't know what to think."

Her mate kissed her cheeks again before pulling back. "Just know that I will always be here for you—even if I wasn't before because of my own inadequacies. My family will always be on your side as well."

"Why do I feel that I'm only strong now because I have you by my side?" she said, finally voicing the thing that had been nagging her.

Maddox let out a dry chuckle, and she narrowed her eyes at him, not understanding what could possibly be humorous at the moment.

"You couldn't be more wrong about that, Ellie mine," he said, his voice adamant. "You've always been resilient on your own. You have to believe that. A mate isn't supposed to take over; they're supposed to join with you and help you become greater than before."

She nodded, not quite believing, but she wouldn't say anything, not yet. She'd have to see for herself if it were true.

"So, we're going to the Centrals to see if we can find their weakness," she said after a moment.

"Goddess, I don't want to take you there. I want to keep you safe," he said, his voice ragged.

"Didn't you just say I was strong and could do anything?"

He snorted. "Yes, and it's the truth, but that doesn't mean I have to like the fact we have to both put ourselves in danger."

"Why do you think Corbin did it?" she asked, unable to say the actual words of what he'd done. Goddess, she couldn't get the sight of their mangled bodies out of her mind, no matter how hard she tried.

"I think it was a message to get the Redwoods' attention," Maddox answered.

"To prove to us that they can get to us no matter what."

Her mate nodded then pulled her into his arms. She sank into his embrace, needing him and his wolf, even if just for the moment.

"They can't get away with it," she whispered. "*He* can't get away with it."

She felt him nod against her, and she inhaled his musky scent, needing to settle down.

"We need to find the person who killed them, but I think they're still with the Pack," Maddox said with an edge.

Ellie pulled back and ran her hands over his shoulders, using touch to calm him, just as he did for her.

"Your family is working on that. Our job was to work through our differences—which we did." She blushed at the memory of just *how* they'd done that. "We also need to find out how they got the mole in. To do that, we need to infiltrate the Centrals as well."

Maddox nodded. "It's time to see what we can do within the Centrals' den instead of the reverse. It's time we see if there's something to be done from our end."

"I don't want to go back. Goddess, I don't want to, but we need to."

Maddox frowned. "I don't want you to get hurt."

"I won't. I mean, it can't be any worse than before." Her jaw snapped shut at her words, and she closed her eyes.

"Ellie, baby, you can tell me what happened. Sometimes the best way to heal is to share. I know I can't help you through my powers as an Omega, but I can listen. And our bond? Yeah, that can help too."

She opened her eyes and smiled wryly. "Is this the same bond that you said would only hurt me?"

He ducked his head. "I was wrong. Can't you feel it? Goddess, you feel so warm, and you're not going crazy over the strength of it."

She smiled. "I can feel you in my head, Maddox. I can feel everything. I know you can feel the muted presence of the Pack through your bond, and I can feel it as well. I can easily see how it could be overwhelming, but I think it'll be different. I think, with the two of us, I can even help you bear that burden."

He stilled for just a moment then relaxed around her. "We'll see when we get home."

Home.

Goddess, everything had changed, hadn't it?

They needed to clear up the past and present first so they could have a future.

"Corbin never raped me," she whispered, saying the words she needed to say before she lost her courage.

Maddox's arms tightened, and she gasped. He relaxed immediately and ran his hands down her back and through her hair.

He swallowed hard and kissed her temple. "Good. Oh, baby, that's good to know."

"He said he'd never go that far. He had his friends rape me repeatedly, but he never joined."

Maddox growled, and she kissed his neck, trying to comfort him.

"I'm going to kill them all, Ellie."

She liked the threat of violence in his voice and licked and nibbled his chin. "You'll have to stand behind me first."

He let out a breath and squeezed her again. "Caym said...before..." He trailed off, and she froze, knowing exactly what Caym had said in the clearing.

"Only a few times," she whispered. "He wanted my brother more, and Corbin gladly gave in."

He kissed her hard, and she lost herself to him. Maddox could take away the hurts, the memories...everything and give so much in return. This was what it meant to be a mate, to relish in the joining and the fullness of having another with you at all times.

"He will die, Ellie. I promise you that. He'll pay for all he's done."

She didn't know if the *he* referred to was Caym or Corbin, or both, but she didn't care. For some reason, no for all the reasons, she believed Maddox and his words.

There had to be a way to end it all, to find peace.

They'd just have to go to the Centrals to start the process. It was time they took the war to them rather than sit back and wait to protect their own.

Goddess, she only hoped she didn't lose more in the process. For now, she had much more to lose.

18

"Ellie, I don't want you to get hurt."

Her eyes closed again at her mate's repeated words, but she didn't say anything. There really was no need. Maddox wanted to lock her up to protect her, but she knew he'd never do it, not when taking away her will would hurt her even more.

"Damn it. I hate this," he grumbled as he packed up the last of their belongings.

They'd start the trek that night to the Centrals' den. It'd be a long journey without a car—it wasn't as if it was just across the street or anything. The dens of the United States were usually surrounded by neutral territories, like the one they stayed in now. Each den was miles wide, the territory even larger—sometimes as big as a state itself. It would take hours to drive to some dens, days even. Even though sometimes it felt like the Centrals were right next door, in reality, their enemy was far away.

They'd make the journey though.

They had to.

Maddox pulled her into his arms and kissed her—hard. He moved back, his breath ragged, and rested his forehead on hers. "I don't like any of this, and though I'm letting you go, I'm not leaving your side."

She smiled at his promise and ran her hands up and down his back. "I'm not leaving your side either. It's just you and me. We're going to go there and find a way to bring them down or at least find out how they infiltrated the Redwoods. We're not going to end the war in one day, goddess no."

He cupped her ass and squeezed. "No, I'd rather them not know we're there at all. This is just for information, nothing more."

She nodded. "Then we'll go home."

"Then we'll go home. We've been gone long enough, almost a week, Ellie. My family has to have something now."

The Jamensons hadn't called since that frantic call from Cailin concerning North. She knew they couldn't. They had to keep the pretenses up that Ellie was banished so Corbin wouldn't attack the den again. Or at least that was their hope.

It was time she and Maddox did something to help beyond finding their own centers. Edward had told them to find a way to protect the Pack, and she was going to do that. Maybe that would even help her in the eyes of the others who doubted her—not because of her own actions but because of who had raised her.

She didn't really blame them though, considering how much the Pack had been through for so long. Death and the burning down of part of their den was enough to put uncertainty and fear in the strongest of wolves.

Maddox pulled her into his arms and kissed her brow. "Let's get on with it then, my Ellie. I might not like what we have to do, but we'll get it done."

She nodded then kissed under this jaw, the stubble scraping against her lips, sending shivers down her back.

Okay, *so* not the time for that.

With one last look at the cabin where everything had changed, she gripped Maddox's hand and sank into the shadows. The path they were taking was as straightforward as they could make it and would only take a day at most if they hurried. Frankly, she didn't want to take her time. She wanted to get it over with, find *something* they could use on the Centrals, and return to her own den where she could get on with her life.

Never before had she thought she'd actually have a future, and she wouldn't give up that hope for anything.

Especially not for a brother who had taken everything from her and had darkened her soul to the point she'd never thought she'd breathe again.

They made good time, talking quietly about things they

had missed over the past two years because they'd hidden their feelings—well, *he* had, her not so much. They ate on the move, not bothering to stop and rest when they knew time was not on their side.

The sound of a branch under an animal's paw made her freeze. The scent of wolf attacked her nose.

Maddox pulled her behind him, the source of the sound in front of them. Her pulse beat in her ears, and she focused on her other senses.

There.

Another wolf.

A Central wolf—or was it?

Maddox squeezed her hand, and she did the same back, and then the other wolf jumped out of the bushes.

The red wolf pounced, its teeth bared, ready to bite into Maddox's arm, but her mate was faster. He pulled her to the side, and she rolled, ready to attack if the wolf came at her and also ready to fight anything else that might come out of the shadows to surprise them.

Maddox stayed in his human form and took the red wolf by the scruff, slamming him down to the ground. He straddled it, forcing it to struggle and it snapped its jaws near Maddox's neck.

Ellie couldn't feel another presence around them no matter how hard she tried and moved to help her mate. She let her wolf rise to the surface, her claws elongating from her fingertips. She hadn't been able to do that type of partial shift when she lived with the Centrals because the action took too much focus, too much strength.

The Redwoods had been good to her in so many ways. She wasn't about to let anyone take that away from her.

When the wolf turned to her, she slashed her claws against its cheek then pressed her claw against its jugular.

"Stop moving," she growled, her wolf howling beneath her skin, loving the feel of power radiating from her.

The wolf glared at her but did as she said.

"Change," Maddox ordered, his voice low, deadly.

The wolf lifted a lip in a snarl, and she pressed her claw harder. A whimper escaped, and the flush of magic brushed against her skin as he changed.

When he was in his human form, she could see the damage to his body she hadn't noticed when he'd been a wolf. Someone had tortured him. Long gashes ran long his sides, and burns covered his body.

The man looked resigned to his fate, and Maddox lifted off him.

"Why did you attack us?" her mate asked.

"You shouldn't be here," the other man rasped out.

"What happened to you?" she asked. Maybe if they knew why he was hurt, they could figure out why he was there.

"Your brother, princess," he said between bouts of coughing.

Maddox growled at the term, but she shook her head.

No use getting mad over her past. They had both been trying to overcome it anyway.

"Why did he do this to you?" she asked.

"Because I failed." The other man winced, his body shaking.

"What did you fail at?" Maddox asked, impatience evident in his tone.

"I killed them like he asked, but the Redwoods didn't kill you. They didn't do anything. They continued to allow your freedom. I failed, and Corbin wasn't pleased."

Ellie blinked.

This man was the one who'd killed Larissa and Neil. The man who'd left those children orphans. The man who had shaken her world right when she'd thought she'd found a way to settle.

Maddox lunged, covering the man again, and this time, her mate's claws came out, sharp and ready to kill.

"Why?"

One word.

One word so deadly, so sharp that Ellie had to hold back a wince. This was her Maddox, not anyone else. That's why she didn't fear him, but, goddess, she'd never heard him sound so lethal.

"He ordered. I obeyed. I failed." He coughed again, this time his whole body convulsing. He lifted his head to look directly into Ellie's eyes. "I'm sorry."

"Sorry you failed or sorry you took their lives?" she asked, a small ball of pity forming in her stomach.

"Sorry I hurt you, princess. I tried to run away with the others when the demon came, but I lost. I'm sorry. My mother was a Redwood so I ended up being both Packs. I know I shouldn't have killed them, but he didn't leave me a choice. I left the den right after so I wouldn't be caught, but Corbin found me. It wasn't enough. It never was enough."

So he was a Central, one who had tried to flee when Caym arrived.

"How did you become a Redwood? That doesn't make any sense."

The wolf wheezed then shook his head. "Corbin told me to come and stay when Caym arrived, after he found out that I tried to run. He wasn't happy. Since my mother was a Redwood, I was allowed in the den." The darkness in his gaze forced Ellie to hold back a shudder. "I'm sorry."

Maddox looked into her eyes, and she sighed. The wolf in front of them was dying. There was no use hiding from it now. His wounds were too severe, and they were no healers. He'd die painfully—much like Neil and Larissa had—but was it their right to allow him to feel that pain? Corbin was the one who had forced this wolf's hand.

The demon and her brother were responsible for all this, not this wolf who had already lost everything and was dying, inflicted with a pain so horrible she didn't want to think about.

"Please..." the wolf whispered. "I know I don't deserve it...but please."

She closed her eyes for a moment then nodded. When

she opened them, her mate frowned but nodded back. Goddess, what right did anyone have to force her mate to do this?

No, she would be the one to do it.

She reached out, but Maddox held her wrist.

"Is there anything else you can tell us?" Maddox asked, his voice kinder than before.

"No, he didn't tell me anything else at all. I'm sorry." Tears slid down the wolf's cheeks, and Ellie bit her lip.

"Go in peace," Maddox whispered then broke the wolf's neck.

It was a quick death, one that the wolf might not have deserved but had been necessary. He hadn't wanted to do anything, hadn't wanted to kill, yet the choice had been taken from him.

"Why didn't you let me handle it, Maddox?" she asked, her voice choked from tears.

He reached out then stopped, looking down at hands that had killed the man lying on the ground.

"You shouldn't have blood on your hands, Ellie mine."

She stood and took his hands, ignoring his wince. "You did what you had to do, and I will do what I have to do. I won't let you put yourself on the line to protect me from something that needs to be done. That man needed peace, and you gave that to him. Now, we know who the mole was, and we need to go back to the den."

Maddox pulled her into his arms. "Let's bury him then go back. We don't know if there were others that came with that first purge. He was so deeply embedded that I couldn't sense who he'd been before. That type of magic worries me."

"We need to talk to your family."

He pulled her into his arms and kissed her softly. His hands, which had just given a peaceful death to the man who'd taken away her safety, held her close. Maddox was her warrior, but he'd just have to deal with the fact she wanted to fight by his side.

Maddox's arms tightened around her as the familiar scent of her nightmares invaded her nostrils.

"Run," he whispered. "Find my family."

Her mate threw her into the shadows and growled.

"No, Maddox."

There was no way she'd leave him.

"Go. Please. It's the only way."

She nodded, her heart thudding in her ears, and then she ran away from the scent of her brother, away from her mate, and toward the Redwoods.

The sound of her mate roaring in pain caused her to stumble.

Dear goddess, what had she done?

MADDOX WOKE to a dark room that seemed eerily familiar. Instead of a bare bulb, harsh florescent lighting burned his eyes. The walls were stained brown and red with blood and goddess knew what else. Large chunks of cement were carved out, as if something much stronger than he had taken siege and tried to escape...or had held back another's attempt.

He tried to move and cursed. Metal dug into his skin at his ankles and thighs. Thick cylinders kept his wrists bound to the table—different from the last time. One chain wrapped around his chest and another at his neck. They dug in as well, leaving a trail of blood where they chafed his skin.

The bastard had chained him to the table and stripped him down to his shorts.

Hell.

He knew this room.

He'd been in this room.

Before it had seemed only yesterday...now it was a lifetime ago, yet he couldn't back away.

The room might have been slightly updated through time, but it still had that same grungy look, same tainted smell. The cloying scent stung his nostrils, and coated his skin as it seeped into his tissues and blood, forever scarring him like the knives he knew his enemy would soon use.

It was only a matter of time.

Corbin had brought him back to the room where he'd first met Ellie—not that Maddox had known it was her at the time. Maddox had saved his brother, his twin, and ended up with the scar that had not only broken him off from reality and his own life, but it had been so deep it had taken a woman with even more scars than he to begin to heal him.

Now, all was lost.

Or, at least, that is what Corbin would think.

Maddox wouldn't be giving up. No, he hadn't last time, not really, and he wouldn't this time. Ellie would get his brothers, even if the journey was long and fraught with danger, and the Jamensons would come for him.

It was past time they took out this piece of trash, this piece of dung that had hurt his Ellie, hurt his mate.

He'd only just locked her in his soul, and he'd be damned if he'd give up now.

The door opened slowly, and Maddox braced himself. He wouldn't show fear to the bastard. No, he wouldn't scream, nor would he plead for mercy. Corbin, Caym, and countless others hadn't shown Ellie mercy, and Maddox wouldn't be the one to beg.

Corbin strode in, that annoying smirk on his face. His dark hair was getting a bit too long, so it hung over his face in lank, sweaty tufts. Maddox remembered Corbin before Caym had shown up, and he hadn't been as skinny, or as sweaty. It looked as if the demon riding him—Maddox inwardly winced at that too-accurate analogy—was taking its toll.

"I wanted my sister, Jamenson, but I'll take you instead." Corbin turned his back to him, as if Maddox wasn't a threat.

Okay, so he wasn't at the moment, but Maddox would kill the bastard later.

"I'll have your twin as well, you know. I'm still vexed after all these years that you lied to me. No matter. I'll just kill you all."

Corbin turned then and smiled, his teeth sharp, his eyes glowing gold.

No, Maddox wouldn't scream this time, no matter what Corbin dealt.

As long as Ellie was safe, nothing else mattered.

19

Ellie's lungs burned as she ran along the edge of the Centrals' wards. The patrols were stringent, uncaring, and brutal. She had to outrun them before they could even scent her. Finally, she found a copse of trees and climbed high into the center tree. The bark dug into her palms, but she didn't care and, frankly, barely felt it.

Goddess, how could she have let Maddox go?

Yes, he'd told her to run toward the Redwoods, but that had been an idiot plan at best.

There was no way she'd have been able to make it to the Redwoods' land in time to save her mate. Then, if she had even gotten there, she'd have had to explain exactly what had happened and *why* she didn't have Maddox by her side. Members of the Pack already didn't trust her, and there was no way she'd let them know she'd left her mate to die.

Bile rose in her mouth, and she swallowed it down,

letting her lungs work normally for the moment while she
caught her breath.

She'd left Maddox to die.

There was really no other way to put it.

He'd forced her to run the opposite direction—had liter-
ally thrown her that way. Yet, she shouldn't have left him.
Everything had happened so fast. One moment they were
slowly coming to terms with the fact that they were
returning home, and in the next moment, the Centrals had
come, and Maddox had sacrificed himself for her.

Damn those Jamenson men and their willingness to
sacrifice themselves.

North had done it, and now so had Maddox. For all she
knew, North lay dead on the Pack grounds because they
hadn't been able to save him in time. Yes, Cailin had called,
but that hadn't told them much.

Maddox could no longer feel his brother along the
Omega bonds, and Ellie couldn't either. It was odd, feeling
these new bonds that had slowly begun to tangle their way
around the center thread that held her to the Pack. She'd
never been able to feel the others in the Pack before—not
when she'd been a Central, nor when she joined the
Redwoods. She'd had a muted bond with Edward, her
Alpha, but nothing as strong as what she felt now.

Now, she could feel her bond to Maddox flaring to life
with each breath—a bond that would surely only
strengthen when they marked each other.

She held back a sob and forced it away at the thought.

It would do no good to cry now, not when she had to figure out a full plan. There was no time for "what-ifs" and she'd just have to put on her brave face and find her mate.

Then they'd mark each other and fully form that bond.

She could only imagine what it would feel like when that happened, not only the connection established when they were fully mated, but also her ability to feel the bonds to the emotions of the Pack. Maddox had once said that he held a thread to each member of the Pack within him. Some threads were thick, unyielding, such as those with his family while others were bare whispers, like those of the members who'd tried to cut themselves off from him.

She didn't know which one he preferred, as the thicker bonds would almost surely overwhelm him and, eventually, her. They were his family and the others who needed help the most. The ones with the thinner threads could also need him and not know it. It was Maddox's job as the Omega to seek those out, ground the bonds, and deepen their emotions.

Goddess, she would be there to help.

There was no way she'd leave him to her brother and the demon that had come to ruin them all.

She'd find her mate, and they would help the others in the Pack because there was no way she'd let him do it on his own anymore.

"We'll save our Maddox," her wolf whispered.

Ellie closed her eyes and let her wolf rise to the surface. She'd hidden her wolf for so long under her brother's and father's bondage, and now she was closer than ever to the spirit that shared her body and her heart.

She blinked once more and tried to tamp down the emotions running rampant through her. It would do no good to wallow in self-pity and self-doubt.

She'd just have to go into the Centrals' den and find him herself. She could do it. After all, she'd grown up there. Though the wards were strong, they weren't perfect. As soon as Caym had come and had tainted everything in his path, the dark wards had become an inky black, suffocating the person who tried to come through without due course. Meaning if she pushed hard enough, she could make it through. Reed and Hannah had done it before and had not alerted the guards, so Ellie would do the same.

Then she'd find Maddox...though she knew where he was. Corbin wasn't that clever with his hiding. No, her brother would want to put Maddox in the same place he'd held him before. Anything that offered a flair for dramatics was Corbin's favorite choice.

Ellie slowly climbed down from the tree and looked over her shoulder for anyone approaching. Her wolf couldn't sense another presence, so Ellie figured she'd be in the clear for the moment.

It was now or never.

Goddess, she just wanted that future with Maddox that she'd finally realized she could have.

She walked up to the dark wards and closed her eyes.

This was going to hurt.

She took a step forward and let the wards surround her. The inky black tugged on her like spindly fingers, curling around her arms and legs, pulling her under, threatening to suffocate her. She took another step then another. There was no way she'd stop, not for anything. The feel of sharp blades against her skin forced her to shake, and sweat rolled down her back, but she continued on. The blades weren't real...she *knew* that.

She kept going, pushing past the pain, the doubts, and the wards that threatened to consume her until she finally made her way through. Abruptly the pain stopped, and she crouched down, opening her eyes at the same time. Again, she couldn't sense anyone, though that didn't surprise her. The Centrals were nothing if not cocky about their wards. While Redwoods knew they couldn't cover their entire den, they worked as a cohesive unit to try and make sure they were safe, but the Centrals took their dark magic for granted.

Goddess, Ellie had no idea how her own soul had survived as long as it had within the Centrals' den, but she was blessed in that regard. She knew if she had stayed any longer, though, she'd have been just as dark as the innocents of the Pack that had been lost.

There was no stopping Caym.

At least not yet.

Ellie made her way to the building at the far corner of the den, ducking behind trees and other buildings as she did so, though she never caught another scent. Corbin's playrooms were in the cement outposts near the edge of the wards. She held back a shudder as memories of just exactly what went on in there flooded through her.

No, she couldn't think about that now.

She needed to get to Maddox.

A wolf prowled in the distance, but she was downwind, and he couldn't sense her. She crept inside the building, her heart racing. She had a feeling she knew what room Maddox would be in—the same one he'd been in all those years ago.

That particular room was the fourth door down, and thankfully, all of the other doors were closed, meaning she could walk past faster. Her feet didn't make a sound against the cement floor as she padded her way to where Maddox was. Yes, she could feel him now, his bond with her pulsing softly. Since they hadn't finished the mating yet, she knew their connection would be erratic, but goddess, she could feel him.

A short burst of relief filled her, but she cut it off. They weren't even close to being safe. She could feel that relief later.

Her mate was just beyond that door, and thankfully, she couldn't sense another. Her wolf whimpered in need, clawing at her skin because she wanted to be with Maddox. Ellie knew exactly how she felt.

Taking a deep breath, she slowly pushed the door open then bit her lip so she wouldn't scream.

Oh, goddess, no.

"Maddox," she whispered.

He lay on the table, his body covered in blood and cuts...just like the last time. Corbin had chained him again and bled her mate until she was afraid that, if she hadn't felt his life through their bond, he'd be no more.

Goddess, they had to get out of there quickly.

She closed the door softly behind her, leaving it open a crack so she could hear if someone was coming, and walked to her mate.

Hesitant to touch him and hurt him any more than he was, she quickly undid his chains, using the key Corbin had left on the table...just out of Maddox's reach.

Her brother loved his mind games.

"Ellie?" Maddox rasped out, his eyes still closed.

"Oh, honey, let's get you out of here," she whispered. "We need to hurry."

"Where are my brothers?" he asked as she sat him up. His body shook at the action, and she wanted to weep for him...then kick her brother's ass.

"We need to go, honey." She knew he was already out of his mind with pain, and she didn't want to add the fact that she'd come alone.

He smiled sadly, his scarred lip tugging. "You came alone, didn't you?"

"Come on, Maddox."

He nodded, as if he didn't believe they'd make it now. Damn man. She'd save him, just like she'd saved the others.

She had to.

"Well well well. I thought you'd show up," Corbin drawled from the doorway, and Ellie froze.

Damn it. She'd been so focused on Maddox she hadn't paid enough attention to the door. Maybe Maddox was right; maybe she wasn't good enough.

Wait, no. Damn it, she was.

"Let us leave, Corbin," she said, her voice surprisingly steady.

"I think not. I'm tired, oh so tired, of dealing with the two of you. It's time we get it over with and let you go on to the other side. It will be easier to take care of the rest of the Redwoods if you're out of the picture."

"Corbin, we can do nothing for you. You don't need us," she said as she slowly moved closer to Maddox. Her mate had his eyes closed, and though he sat up on the table, he was leaning on her heavily. She could feel his heart beating and held back a sigh of relief.

"You're everything!" Corbin yelled then smiled that cruel smile that would haunt her nightmares until the day she died. "No, I'm wrong. You *used* to be everything. That's why you'll die by my hands now. I've found another...toy."

Ellie froze then finally saw the little girl standing behind Corbin. She wore a collar around her neck that was attached to a large chain that Corbin held.

Like a pet.

Oh, goddess.

Ellie's wolf perked up then growled, letting the scent of this little girl wash over her.

There was something familiar about her...something...
oh, goddess.

Corbin's eyes narrowed, and he smirked again. "Ah, I see
you know her. Or, at least you know who she is."

"But how?"

"This is Hector's bastard." He tugged at the chain, and
the little girl stumbled into the room. "Seems our dear
father found a second mate but didn't tell anyone. Apparently, he didn't want me knowing. Hell, he thought I was
crazy. Why the hell would he think that?"

She knew Corbin wasn't alone—or at least he'd be an
idiot if he was. There was no way she could protect an
injured Maddox, a little girl who probably didn't trust her,
and herself all at once. Corbin threw his head back and
laughed, and Ellie stopped herself from killing the
bastard.

Maddox gripped her hand, holding her back, as though
reading her mind.

"In case you were wondering, this little bitch is Charlotte, and, apparently, five years ago Hector got busy with
her momma and hid her away, outside the Pack."

There was no sickly sweet smell on the girl, meaning
she was clear of the evil. So that's how the little girl survived
the taint, but Ellie knew the little girl wouldn't last long, not
staying with Corbin and most likely Caym.

Goddess, she had a sister.

A helpless sister that she couldn't save...not yet.

"I'd been saving Charlotte to use to sharpen my knives,

but now that you've pissed me off one last time, I won't hold myself back."

Ellie growled, and Maddox joined her.

"Take me instead," Ellie said, knowing it was the only thing she could do. She'd do anything for Maddox, and now also this little girl who was her blood.

Maddox growled again. "No, take me. Let the girls go."

Her heart broke, shattering into a thousand pieces, so many pieces that no one would be able to put her back together again, at the thought of losing him when she'd just found him.

Corbin merely smiled. "Aw, you guys make my teeth ache, but no. I don't want one as damaged as either of you. I like my pristine white canvas."

He cupped Charlotte's chin, and Ellie lost it, running and jumping on Corbin with her teeth bared, her claws out.

Corbin pushed the little girl to the side and raised the gun she hadn't seen or smelled, and fired. A searing burn flared across her shoulder, and she hit the ground, rolling to her feet. She didn't stop, though. She barreled into him. She must have surprised him because he dropped the gun, and she caught it. She turned it on him and fired, only to be knocked to the ground by another wolf she didn't know had been nearby.

She heard, rather than saw, Maddox limp toward her, his growl sending shivers down her spine. He pulled the wolf off her and broke its neck.

Corbin lay on the ground, alive but bleeding. He

growled at her and tried to get up, only to have Charlotte kick him in the neck.

"Come on, Charlotte, come with me," Ellie said through gritted teeth. Goddess, she hurt.

"Caym has the key," the little girl whispered. "I'm chained to Corbin, but Caym has the key."

"Then I'll cut the bastard's arm off," Maddox growled.

The scents of at least forty wolves and Caym came at her, and she cursed. "They're coming, Maddox."

Footsteps echoed in the hall, and tears stained Ellie's cheeks. "How do we get her? Come on, let's cut off his arm." She reached to do so and the bomb blew.

She hadn't even known there was one to begin with.

The blast threw her from Charlotte and into Maddox who screamed in pain as they hit the wall. Part of the ceiling crashed down in front of them, blocking her path.

Goddess, no. She couldn't make it over the debris and save Maddox at the same time.

Corbin woke then and growled, pulling Charlotte into his arms, his hand precariously around her neck over her collar. "Come at me, and I'll kill her."

Maddox reached out and took her hand.

Oh, goddess. They'd have to leave her, or they'd all die.

She looked into Charlotte's eyes, and the little girl nodded. She couldn't tell Charlotte her plans to come back, not with Corbin right there, but goddess, the look of pain and...nothing...in that little girl's gaze.

Maddox's legs gave out, and she pulled her bleeding mate into her arms and ran, leaving her sister behind.

Goddess, that hurt. How could she choose between her mate and the sister she'd never known existed?

She pulled her mate down the path they'd taken all those years before when she'd saved him, her shoulder burning, and tears running down her cheeks.

She'd be back.

She had to be.

20

"Hold still," North growled as he pressed the gauze pad to Maddox's side.

Maddox winced but moved again, needing to keep his eyes on Ellie. He'd never let her leave his sight if he had a choice.

His mate sat on the couch in front of him, a frown on her face as Hannah Healed her. There was no way he'd let Ellie get far from him in his current state—or any state in the near future for that matter.

Gods, when Corbin had lifted up his arm and shot Ellie...

Maddox bit his tongue so he wouldn't scream. He wanted to jump up and grab his mate so he could hold her and never let go. She'd shot the bastard in the side and would have killed him if that other wolf hadn't jumped on her and knocked her off her aim.

If only Maddox had been able to move faster, then it all might have been over.

North poked and prodded a deep cut on his side, and Maddox cursed. Well, hell, that's why he hadn't been able to move. It was a miracle he'd been able to do what he'd done in the first place, considering the amount of deep cuts and gashes he had over his body. Corbin had also used the cursed knife, adding pain and scars to his body. Due to the blast, they each had a couple broken bones and who knew what else.

As long as Ellie was safe, though, he'd take any scar the bastard gave him.

"This cut is deep, Mad," North mumbled. "You should have Hannah look at it. You *should* have had Hannah take care of it to begin with. That's why we have a Healer."

Maddox tore his gaze from his bleeding mate and glared at his twin, who looked no worse for wear from his chest wound—thank the goddess.

"As soon as Ellie is Healed, I'll happily let Hannah help me if she has the strength," Maddox said then turned toward Ellie again, unable to part from her for even that long.

Hannah cocked a brow while keeping her hands on Ellie, the feel of magic filling the room as she Healed his mate.

"I'm going to be okay, Mad," Ellie whispered, and he nodded, though they both knew she wouldn't be okay with the choice she'd made.

The choice she'd had to make because of him.

They'd walked back, bleeding and in pain, to a checkpoint where the Redwoods had taken them into the den. The Centrals hadn't followed them, either because of the blast or because they hadn't cared enough. Rather than sending them to North's clinic, they'd gone directly to his father's house, where Hannah and North had come to them.

Apparently, his father had already been in Alpha-mode talking to Lexi and Logan, who were also in the room with them. Oddly enough, so was Cailin, who stood scowling in the corner, her wolf right at the surface.

What was even odder was that, though he could feel what they were feeling—rage, sadness, confusion, and so much more—it wasn't as bad as it usually was.

Goddess, what if he'd been wrong all this time?

What if mating with Ellie fully would actually *help* him control his powers?

Hell, he'd have to talk with her because, if she was feeling what he felt, she'd be okay, and they would be able to live like that...maybe, but if she was actually taking *all* the emotions he should have been feeling then they'd have to find a way to fix that.

Soon.

Out of the corner of his eye, he saw Lexi move closer to North, an oddly pained look on her face as she handed him the last of the bandages that North would use on Maddox's side. Maddox had a feeling that look had to do with North himself, but it wasn't his place to get in the middle of whatever the hell was going on.

At least for now that is.

North was his twin, after all, and he'd inserted himself directly into Maddox and Ellie's mating from the beginning. Yes, he should, at some point, thank the bastard for helping Ellie through her first insertion into the pack when Maddox had been an idiot and unable to do it himself, but it would take time for his wolf to get over the fact that North had been so close to his mate for so long.

Even if, technically, it was Maddox's fault to begin with.

Logan stood behind Lexi, scowling at everyone, as if he'd protect his sister no matter the cost. Parker, thankfully, wasn't in the room. He was in another one with Josh and Reed helping with the twins. Apparently, Edward had gotten close to the boy and had trusted—or at least saw the beginnings of trust—the ex-Talons as soon as he'd met them.

It didn't come as too much of a surprise to Maddox, considering how he, North, and Ellie had also found that connection easy to make with the trio.

Logan shot a look at Cailin and frowned then tore his gaze away again to look at Lexi.

Well. Interesting.

Jealousy, confusion, and a not-so-little amount of lust spread from Cailin to Logan and back again, forcing Maddox to blink.

Hell, his little sister might have just found her mate.

He held back a smile. There was no way this would go easy, and from the looks of things, North and Lexi wouldn't have an easy time either. The two didn't seem to be talking to one another and the tension radiating from them was so thick he could taste it.

Thank the goddess he had Ellie.

At that thought, he did smile. Things sure had changed since he'd left the den with North and Ellie in tow to figure out how they would make it through being in the same den in pain. Now, North and Maddox would find a way to fix the bonds that might have frayed, and Maddox had his Ellie.

Or at least he'd have her fully as soon as they dealt with the Pack politics that needed to be discussed before they left the house.

His father paced the room. His mother was out on patrol with the rest of his brothers. There were short on enforcers now, and there was no way anyone would go alone. Everything had changed since Caym had come to their plane, yet the Redwoods wouldn't back down.

They *wouldn't* back down.

"Tell us what happened, son," his Alpha ordered. "We know what happened with North and these three, but tell us what happened after you were alone with Ellie."

Maddox met Ellie's gaze as she blushed, and he winked, smiling again.

"Hell, I don't think I've seen you smile like that before, Mad," Cailin said from her corner. "Way to go, Ellie."

Maddox let out a small growl, and Ellie blushed harder. "Stop it, little sister."

"Enough you two," Edward said. "Tell us."

So, Maddox told them about the attack, the traitor they'd killed, and his torture, leaving out the details of certain events. His family could tell he and Ellie were partially mated by their scents, and his father could tell by their bond. There was no need to mention it. He also wasn't about to tell them exactly what had happened in the dungeon. North and Hannah were in the process of Healing the evidence of it that Ellie had sustained. So Maddox wasn't about to make them live through it with him.

He might tell Ellie while they were alone because, for some reason, he needed her to know everything about him, just as he needed to know everything about her.

That's what it meant to be mates.

To live through the bad, the ugly, and everything so much worse, so they could cherish the good.

He also left out Charlotte for the time being. He'd tell them all soon, but first, he needed to get a few things out of the way before his family got in an uproar over the child. His wolf growled at the thought of what could be happening at the moment.

He couldn't think about it.

Damn it, he'd save the child as soon as he was on his feet and they were able to leave. There was no way they'd let Charlotte stay in Corbin's clutches.

"The traitor is dead then," Edward said under his breath

before walking to Ellie's side. "We never believed you did it, Ellie dear. You know this."

She looked up at her Alpha, and Maddox held back the urge to move and tug her into his arms.

"I know," she whispered as Hannah left her side to Heal Maddox.

Maddox shook his head as his brother's mate Healed his wounds, the magic flowing through him, making him feel warm and sleepy.

"Do you?" Edward said, his voice softer than Maddox had thought possible for his father.

"Yes, through it all, I knew the Jamensons believed in me. It was the others. They never did trust me. I'm a Central."

Edward growled, his Alpha power filling the room with a quick snap. "No, you are not. You are a Redwood."

Maddox growled back at his father's tone, despite the words, but cut off when Ellie gave him a look. Yes, he knew she needed to stand up for herself, but damn, it was hard to sit back and let her be on her own.

"I know," Ellie said, her voice calm. "I misspoke. I know I'm a Redwood. I love this Pack."

"Good. You're a Jamenson now, Ellie dear. That thick-headed son of mine finally figured out what was in front of him this whole time and brought you into our fold. We're never letting you go now, dear."

She smiled, and Maddox felt a burst of love and acceptance through their bond.

"We've always stood by you, Ellie," his father continued. "We've always told and *shown* the others you were part of us, but you had to go so we could ferret out the traitor and so Corbin would think we'd forced you out. Now, we need to all stand strong and show the Pack that you're not only one of us but you're also family. You're the Omega female, Ellie. You're Pack."

She bowed her head, and the rest of the people in the room, even the ex-Talons, did the same.

When the Alpha spoke, his word was law.

There would be no second chances with those in the Pack who had doubted his Ellie.

None.

"So, the bastard that killed Neil and Larissa is dead?" Cailin asked, the anger in her tone beating down on him with each breath.

Maddox met her gaze and nodded. "Yes, he'd dead." *By my own hands.* He'd have to talk that out with Ellie like so many things he'd done in his past, but that was for another time.

"I know it's fair to call that man a killer, but it wasn't all his responsibility," Ellie cut it.

Maddox held out his hand, and she walked to him, her gaze for only him. He pulled her down on his lap, pressing his nose against the part where her shoulder met her neck, needing to scent her and make sure she was real...that she was okay. He ignored the pointed glances of the others in the room. They'd just have to get used to this new him. After all, he was just getting used to it himself.

"What do you mean by that?" North asked. He moved to stand against the wall, Lexi near him but not touching.

"Corbin was the one who ordered it," Ellie said. "Caym was the one whose evil incarnation tainted the bonds within their Pack and forced them to do things."

Maddox pressed her to his chest, feeling her heart speed up as she spoke—either from the subject matter or the fact that her body was so close to his.

"I'm glad you got out when you did," Hannah said, leaning into Edward's side.

Maddox's father was nothing if not fatherly and caring to all his kids—even those mated in.

"And, if anyone thinks that you've been tainted by their magic, they just have to look at you and see who you truly are," North said, causing Maddox to growl softly.

North held up his hands and shook his head. "I meant nothing by it."

"They'll have to go through me if they want to hurt her," Maddox said, his voice still a growl.

Ellie turned in his lap and kissed his lips softly. "We'll be okay, Maddox. You don't have to punch everyone who looks at me weird."

Maddox frowned at that. "They shouldn't be looking at you weird—or at all for that matter. You're mine."

"It's about time," his wolf said.

Damn wolf.

"If you're so worried about people looking at your mate, maybe you should mark her to make it public," his father said pointedly.

He could feel the heat of Ellie's pretty blush rush to her skin, and he kissed that fleshy part of her shoulder where he'd mark her later.

"Soon," he said, leaving it at that. There was no need to let everyone know he was planning on taking her out of the house soon and marking her as his.

Slowly at first, then maybe fast and hard later.

Or, maybe the reverse of that.

His wolf growled, and his cock filled. Ellie froze on his lap, and he held back a groan. Yep, no hiding that from her, but first they had to deal with the one thing they hadn't talked about...the one thing that he knew that could break them if they let it.

"We found one other thing at the Centrals'," Maddox said, and Ellie growled. He had put it off because he knew they'd ignore everything else for the little girl—as they should. Also, he had a feeling it wouldn't be as easy as he'd like to go get her.

Good, he'd rather have her experiencing anger at the situation than see the broken look she'd had when they'd left the Centrals' den.

"There was a girl..." Ellie began and shook her head.

"Apparently, Hector had a daughter with his second mate that no one knew about," Maddox put in when it looked like Ellie wouldn't be speaking.

"Oh, goddess," Hannah said and reached out to take Ellie's hand. His mate gripped Hannah's hand, and Maddox kissed her neck again.

"I won't go into it all, but we need to get her out of there now," Maddox said.

"I take it your sister is clear of the taint," Edward said. A statement, not a question.

"Yes, she's clear. Neither of us scented or felt it on her. She also wasn't raised in the den so isn't in the same realm as the others. We need to save her. She's only five." A shudder rippled through Ellie, and Maddox squeezed her tighter.

"Then let's go get her," Cailin said as she rolled her shoulders. "We can't let your little sister stay with that bastard. No offense to you."

"None taken," Ellie said. "I would have killed him right then and there if it hadn't been for that damn wolf coming out of nowhere. Then the bomb..."

"He'll be waiting for us," Edward said, his voice oddly calm.

"So?" Maddox said. "We can't leave that little girl there. She's family."

"Yes, I know this, but as Alpha, I can't order you to go. Nor would it be good to order you to stay."

Ah, Maddox understood. As Alpha, his dad couldn't tell them to risk their lives for someone who technically wasn't Pack. If, however, Maddox left on his own accord, that would be a different matter.

"Cailin, you cannot go," Edward put in, and Cailin growled, her anger filling the room in a violent fury that set Maddox's teeth on edge. Ellie too shuddered again.

"What?" Cailin asked, her body shaking.

"You heard me," Edward said. "I won't hear another word about it."

He knew his father was protecting his only daughter, but one day he'd go too far trying to hold her in, and she'd break. He only hoped that someone would be there to pick up the pieces...like maybe this Logan of hers.

"I'm taking Ellie home," he said. "We need to rest."

Edward nodded. "Be careful, son."

They said goodbye to the others, and he tangled his fingers with Ellie's as they walked toward his home. They hadn't talked about it, but since she didn't have more than a small area to live in, it only made sense that she'd stay with him.

They also hadn't had a chance to talk to the ex-Talons at length. There would be time to talk about everything and what their plans were soon.

Right now, he needed Ellie.

"I just realized you said home back there," Ellie said as she leaned into him, her body stiff with tension.

"Yes, was that not okay?" He rubbed his thumb along her forefinger, needing to keep touching her.

"Yes, oh, yes. We just hadn't talked about it, you know?"

He opened his front door and led her into his home. It wasn't decorated very well and needed a woman's touch, though he'd left it thinking he'd never have that. Now, he had Ellie here, in a place that could be called her own, as well.

"I'm sorry. I should have realized it before I said it." He pulled her into his arms and kissed her softly. Her lips were smooth and oh so soft. Goddess, he loved this woman...he just had to say it.

"I know," Ellie said. "We were scared before, but now... Now I don't want to go back. I don't want to forget what happened in the cabin. I only want to move forward. I want to find Charlotte and bring her here, Maddox. She doesn't have much time. Even if Corbin lets her live, he might not let the evil stay away for long."

He nodded, understanding. "We will, and we'll raise her, Ellie. She'll know what it means to have family. She'll be safe."

Tears filled her eyes, and she kissed him hard. His cock pressed against her belly, and he groaned into her mouth.

"I love you, Ellie mine, and I'm never letting you go. I was such a fucking idiot before, but I'm never going back. Just like you said, it's up to us to look forward, and that's what I'm going to do." He framed her face with his hands and kissed her again. "I love you. I love you. I love you."

She gave a wobbly smile and kissed him back. "I love you, Maddox. I love you so freaking much, and I don't want to wait to mate any longer. I know you're scared of the bond and what it will do to me, but I can feel the Pack, Maddox. I can feel what they're feeling, and it's not too much. I know it'll be more when our wolves are mated, but I don't care. Our wolves *need* this. *We* need this. With the two of us, we can do it together and make it even better. I know it."

Maddox smiled, the tug on his lip from his scar reminding him that life was too short to hide as he had for so long.

"All right."

Her eyes widened. "That's it? After all that brooding of yours, you're ready?"

"I don't brood."

She blinked. "Maddox, baby, you're the epitome of a brooding mate, but I love you anyway."

He laughed and tugged her closer. "We're going to find your sister soon, baby, but first I want to make sure we're fully mated. We don't have much time and if we go into the enemy's den again without being fully mated, we might lose something. With the bond we can be stronger and be able to fight harder. We need this. I know it's not the time, but we need this."

His wolf growled, sending vibrations along his skin, and Ellie gasped, her eyes darkening. "Yes, please."

Maddox nipped at her lips. "You never have to beg for me to want you, Ellie mine." He tugged at her hair, forcing her head back, and he took her lips in a hard, possessive kiss. He would never tire of her taste, her touch, her everything.

Their tongues tangled, and he licked at her mouth, kissing up her neck until he began to nibble. "I'm going to sink my fangs into this pretty skin of yours, baby. All other males will know you're mine. And when you do the same to me, I'm going show off your mark, letting everyone know I'm just as much yours."

"Okay, but first, I want to try something." She gave him a little coy smile that caused his dick to throb.

She slowly knelt before him, letting her nails scratch lightly over his clothes as she did so. She looked up at him, her dark eyes wide and that pretty little tongue licking her lips.

"I want to taste you. You didn't let me last time."

He groaned and shook his head, running his hand through her hair. "You don't need to, baby."

"I know, but I want to."

"Hell, I'm the luckiest man in the world right now."

She smiled and undid his pants, pulling them and his boxers down below his knees. His cock sprang out, and she moved back.

He swallowed hard as she studied his dick, running her fingers tentatively along the length then down to cup his balls. He sucked in a breath and tightened his grip in her hair.

"I don't know what to do," she whispered, that pretty blush filling her cheeks.

He cupped her chin and forced her to look at him, running his thumb along that smooth blush of hers. "Do anything you want, baby. I'm all yours."

"Yay for me," she said.

Maddox's eyes about crossed as she licked the head and seam, stroking as she tightly gripped the base.

"Hell," he muttered.

She stopped and looked up. "Not good?"

He ran his hand through her hair again. "So fucking good, baby."

She smiled then swallowed the head of his cock, letting her tongue trace around it as she did so.

Oh, holy goddess.

Ellie's cheeks hollowed as she swallowed as much of him as she could, rolling his balls in her palm as she stroked him with her other hand.

He held back as best he could, sweat rolling down his back as he forced himself not to thrust into her pretty mouth. She bobbed her head as she took him in and out of her mouth, letting her tongue dance along his cock.

His Ellie looked up at him, and he about blew. Goddess, she was so fucking pretty with her dark eyes and those pretty lips wrapped around his cock. How the hell had he gotten so lucky?

He pulled out, and she frowned.

"I wasn't finished."

He pulled her up to a standing position and crushed his mouth to hers. "I know, baby, but I want to come inside that sweet pussy of yours. We have lifetimes for me to come down your throat."

She ducked her head and blushed even harder. "Who knew you'd talk so dirty."

He smiled and bit her chin. "I didn't know I would either. You just bring it out of me. Don't worry, baby, I'll teach you to talk dirty too."

She smiled back. "I'm not afraid of what you and I do together, not anymore. I want to do *everything*, Maddox."

Images of every position they could do and feeling they could have flooded his mind, and he had to grip his cock hard so he wouldn't come.

"Hell, Ellie mine. Tell me what you want first."

She bit her lip and looked to be deep in thought. "Hmm, can you take me from behind? I really, really want to try that."

He threw his head back and laughed, even as he almost came once again. "Hell yeah, we can do that. I have an idea, baby."

He kicked off his shoes and pants and led her to the living room. There, he shucked off his shirt and tore off her clothes, the sound of ripping fabric echoing in the room.

"Hey! I don't have many clothes, you know," she said with a laugh.

He kissed her hard again. "I'll buy you as many as you want. Later."

He ran his hands up and down those smooth curves of hers and over her scars. She didn't even wince this time, and he wanted to howl in triumph.

"Do you trust me?" he asked, knowing that if she hesitated at all he'd take the hurt because he knew they still had time. He also wouldn't be as rough as he wanted at the moment and take it slow.

Anything for his Ellie.

"Of course."

No hesitation, just a promise.

He ran his hands down her sides again then turned her around so she faced the couch.

"Bend over for me, baby. You said you wanted it from behind."

She looked over her shoulder then bent over, baring that sweetness for him. He nudged her legs apart, and then he ran kisses over her ass then to her pussy.

Fuck, she tasted like heaven.

He licked up her juices, and she squirmed against his face.

"Maddox..." she whispered.

He didn't stop, just kept licking around her clit then using his fingers to spread her wide, letting his tongue dip in and out until they were both panting with need.

Maddox's fingers traced her pussy, and then he thrust them in, reaching that bundle of nerves that made Ellie's legs shake so hard he had to push her harder against the couch. He rubbed and circled until her pussy clenched around his fingers and she screamed his name. Before her body stopped shaking, he stood up, gripped her hips, and slammed into her.

He froze as she threw her head back, her ass against his body, his cock balls deep in her pussy.

"Shit," he whispered, willing his cock not to explode after that first stroke. Her inner walls were still vibrating from her last release, and fuck, she was tight.

And his.

"Please, please, Maddox," she begged as she wiggled her ass, and he couldn't hold back anymore.

He slid out of her slowly then rammed back into her hard, repeating the thrust over and over until all he could do was feel her around him and listen to the sounds of their bodies slamming into each other, their breathing heavy and laden with lust.

He reached around and pulled her flush against his chest, his hands sliding up to cup her breasts. He licked and sucked her neck, her head lolling to the side to give him more access. His hips worked maniacally as he fucked his mate with everything he had.

His fangs popped out of his gums, his wolf ready to mark and be with his mate in every way possible.

"Mark me. Please, for the love of God, stick those fangs in me as...as I ride your cock."

He sucked in a breath at the way she talked dirty and smiled.

"As you wish, Ellie mine."

With that, he thrust hard, his body flush against hers, and he sank his fangs into her shoulder, marking her as his in all ways possible. He came as she did, her pussy clenching around him, fluttering and draining his cock as he spilled his seed. He gave a few shallow thrusts, letting her ride out her orgasm, and he could feel his cum, wet and heady around his flesh.

He lifted his fangs and licked up the wound.

Fuck, that mark looked delectable.

He sucked on the mark and groaned as her pussy clenched again.

His wolf howled in pleasure as the bond slowly started to take root, though it wasn't over yet, not by far.

He pulled out, and Ellie whimpered. He leaned down and kissed her mark then turned her around to take her lips.

"We're not through yet, baby."

"But, you already came," she said, her voice drunk with pleasure.

"I'm a wolf, darling. We can go again. And we will because I need those fangs of yours in my neck. Now."

She smiled, and he picked her up, practically running to his—no, *their*—bedroom.

He set her on the bed—carefully—then pulled her hair away from her neck to admire his work.

She raised a brow at him. "Really? You look like a rooster in a hen house right now."

He just grinned, that scar tugging on his lip, but he didn't care. "Sounds about right. You look so fucking good with my mark on you. Now, let's see how you mark me."

Her eyes glowed gold, and she smiled.

He threw himself on the bed and gripped her so she had

to straddle him. "Do anything you want to me, baby. I'm yours."

She smiled again and nodded. "That is the best thing ever. I can't believe I get to have you."

He pulled her palms to him then kissed the center of each softly. "I'm sorry it took so long to happen, but we're not looking back. This is it. This is *us*."

She nodded then lifted her hips, reaching down to position his cock at her entrance. Then she looked into his eyes and slowly slid down him.

Hell.

Sweet hell.

She rode him like a goddess, her hips rotating as she figured out exactly what she wanted. He just held onto her hips to keep her steady and fell in love all over again with that lush skin of hers.

Finally, she leaned down, taking his lips in a sweet kiss, then trailed her tongue down his neck.

"Mark me as yours," he whispered, needing her now more than ever.

"Forever," she said against his neck, her teeth grazing him.

"Forever," he agreed.

She bit down, and he was lost.

He came as she did, an explosion of need, sex, heat, and everything in between. Their bond flared and grew before cementing into this new idea of who they were—who they could be together.

His wolf howled again as it found its own mate, and Maddox smiled against Ellie's hair. Her body lay spent along his as his cock still filled her.

Goddess, this was what he'd needed his whole life, and he'd be damned if anyone tried to take it away. The world would still be out there tomorrow, and he and Ellie would find a way to mend the hurts and pains, but right now, it was all about the two of them.

He'd found his mate, and nothing would break this new fragile bond.

Nothing.

21

"I almost wish I could still feel the Pack bonds so I could find her," Ellie whispered then suppressed a shudder at the thought of still being connected to the Centrals.

Maddox and Ellie had passed through the wards already, the memory of the pain in doing so a distant memory. She wasn't sure if people not connected to the Centrals by old bonds and being mated to those old bonds would have made it through. The inky black wards were as strong as ever, but she didn't care. They'd made it through, and now they were waiting behind a grouping of rocks so they could figure out where the best place to find Charlotte was.

Goddess, she hoped the little girl was okay.

Considering whom they'd been forced to leave her with, Ellie wasn't so sure.

Another shudder racked her body, and Maddox pulled

her closer to him, his lips or chin brushing the top of her head. She took a deep breath and tried not to let her memories and imagination get the better of her.

They'd save her little sister before it was too late.

There really wasn't another option.

Not only did Ellie want to make sure Corbin couldn't touch a hair on her pretty little head, but she also wanted to ensure Caym couldn't get his claws into Charlotte. The little girl's soul only had so much time until the evil would take root and all would be lost. Even then, she didn't know how long the little girl had been there. Goddess, there wasn't much time.

There was no way she'd let that happen.

Ellie had already lost one sister and a cousin that had been as good as a sister to her.

She wouldn't lose another.

She *couldn't* lose another.

Maddox's lips brushed her ear, and she took a deep breath.

"We'll find her, Ellie mine. As for the bonds you want back, I know you're just frustrated. You don't need those to find her. We already know where she's likely to be."

She nodded, leaning into him more and inhaling that musky scent that reminded her she wasn't alone anymore.

No, she didn't want those bonds anymore. Now, she not only had the bonds to her Pack, but the one to Maddox that was thriving—alive and pulsating with each breath and thought.

Not only could she feel exactly what Maddox was feeling—something that not all mates could do—she could also do the same to the Pack. Some mates could feel some feelings and some relative positions, but it depended on the mated pair on how strong that was. Before all of this, Maddox couldn't feel her emotions through his Omega powers, but now it came through in full force.

The connections to the Pack grew and stabilized with each passing moment. It wasn't a huge barrage of feelings that could overwhelm her. She could feel their anger, their confusion, their love, their...everything, but she could also feel the emotions flow between her and Maddox. It was what she'd thought—what she'd hoped for. They shared each other's burdens.

That morning she'd woke in his arms and inhaled his scent for a blissful moment before life had crashed in. She'd known they couldn't wait for their bodies and bonds to heal and form any longer. They had to go out and find Charlotte.

Now, they were here, not precisely against Edward's wishes, but darn close to it. They hadn't brought any of the others to help them because they needed to be as quiet as possible. Too many wolves and they might have alerted the Central wolves. They would have loved to have others fight by their side, and Ellie knew the Jamensons would have come, but they hadn't been able to.

Just the idea that she had a family now that would risk their lives for someone they had never met made her want to scream in happiness. She'd never had that before, and now she had almost everything she wanted.

Almost.

Goddess, she just wanted this to be over, but she didn't think it would be any time soon.

Maddox's words finally registered, and she turned to kiss under his chin.

"She's in his dungeon. That's the only place I think he'd have her now. He might have hidden her away before, but now that he's truly pissed at us..."

Her words trailed off because she was unable to say what could be going on.

Maddox held her tightly, their wolves rubbing against their skin. She only knew Maddox's wolf was at the surface because of their bond and the way her wolf growled at the closeness.

"Let's go," he whispered, and she nodded.

They quickly ran, darting behind trees as they went, toward the dungeon.

When they made their way out of this, she'd do everything in her power to avoid stepping foot in this building again. Goddess, she hated it, but her innocent sister was locked away, and there wasn't a choice.

They walked down the empty hall and made their way to the room Ellie thought Charlotte would be in. Just like before, there were no guards. The Centrals didn't guard this building as much as the other ones since this was for Corbin's fun, not anything else. After all, it had been Ellie's room for so long when she'd been a child. It had been where the beatings had taken place... the torture. The rapes had been in other rooms. Ellie just hoped this is where Charlotte would be.

She couldn't feel another adult wolf around her, only a small presence that had to be a child. She let out a breath, and Maddox slowly opened the door, which caused a creak.

Oh praise the goddess.

Charlotte still wore a collar, but it was different. Ellie recognized it because it was one Ellie herself had worn in what seemed like a lifetime ago. Charlotte was chained to the wall, sitting on the floor but otherwise looked unharmed. She stood when Ellie entered.

The little girl's eyes widened. "You came back," she whispered.

Tears slid down Ellie's cheeks, but she brushed them away, not wanting to scare the child.

"Yes, we came back," she said in a low voice. "We need to go now though. Will you come with me and my mate, Maddox?" Once they found the key that had her chained. Goddess, they needed to *move*.

Charlotte looked between the two of them and looked as though she was fighting with herself. Ellie couldn't blame the child. After all, she knew only that Ellie was her sister, but Corbin was also her brother. Who knew what the child could be thinking?

Maddox took a step inside, his palms raised. "We won't hurt you, Charlotte."

The little girl blinked and nodded.

The relief that swept through Ellie was short lived, however.

Four guards rushed in, and Ellie turned, her claws out, ready to fight. Maddox turned as well, his eyes gold with rage, and he growled.

The guards attacked, and Ellie jumped on the closest one, her claws tearing through flesh along his side. It didn't matter that these men had once been her Packmates. There were no longer, and even before, they'd done nothing to help her.

In fact the two that fought her now had also taken her innocence.

Something they would pay dearly for.

She roared and slashed her claws down one of the bastard's neck. His eyes widened, and he gripped the wound, blood pouring out of him. She kicked him in the stomach, and he fell to his knees. He wouldn't be healing from that neck wound since she'd cut his jugular, so she kicked him again and turned to face the other one that had taken so much from her.

"I'm going to fuck you like I did all those times before, you bitch. Then, when that little bitch behind you is older, I'll fuck her, too." The bastard continued to taunt her, but she let it roll off her.

She wasn't chained down like she'd been before. No, now she was strong and free.

Something this wolf would never understand.

Maddox roared again as he killed his second guard and launched himself toward them. She knew he'd heard what the wolf had said, but this was her fight. She shook her head, and Maddox stopped, seeming to understand her need to take care of this on her own.

The other wolf jumped at her then, and she ducked out of the way, falling to her knees but coming back up again near Corbin's tools. With one quick movement, she picked up a sharp knife and twisted on one foot, burying the knife to the hilt in the guard's neck.

He seemed surprised for a moment, and then like his friend, he fell to his knees.

She twisted the knife then pulled it out, watching as the life faded from her tormentor's eyes.

"You'll never have me again. Ever," she whispered as he died.

Ellie looked up at her mate and saw the love and admiration in his eyes. He'd let her fight for herself, yet she'd known he'd be there if she'd needed him.

This was just another reason why she loved the man.

"Touching, really fucking touching," Corbin drawled from the doorway. "I'm not surprised you're back for the little wolf. I *am* surprised you two came alone. It's as if you *want* to die by my hands. Something that can be arranged."

Corbin lunged then, apparently done talking. His claws were out, and Maddox jumped forward. Their bodies crashed against each other as Maddox pushed Corbin into the wall. Ellie ran to help her mate but hit the ground as two more wolves entered the room, pouncing on her.

She kicked the nearest wolf, ignoring its whimper, then stabbed the one above her with the knife she still held. The weight of the wolf burned her arms, but she pushed it off then scrambled to her feet as four more wolves entered the room, their teeth bared, their souls just as black as the others. The darkness that seeped from them was so blatant, that anyone could have seen it; felt it.

Goddess, they were outnumbered.

However, she and Maddox were stronger than the other wolves because they hadn't been eaten away day by day by a magic that was darker than anything she knew. Only Corbin and Caym were stronger, and she had a feeling Corbin was only stronger because of Caym himself.

She tamped down the fear that threatened to take hold and charged, taking down one wolf with her knife to its chest. She ducked to the ground and rolled, slicing another wolf at its paws. Another wolf jumped on top of her, and she twisted, trying to get away. The wolf clawed at her, and she screamed but didn't stop moving.

The weight was lifted off her as Maddox picked up the wolf and threw it into the wall. The crack of its back breaking echoed into the room, and it whimpered. Maddox pulled her to her feet, and she nodded, not able to do anything more than be glad he was alive.

She glanced at Charlotte who hid behind a table, huddling, tears running down her face.

Maddox turned toward Corbin again and started at him, his fists flying. More wolves poured into the room, and she went on autopilot, fighting as hard as she could. Out of the corner of her eye, she saw her mate fighting. He was a thing of beauty, his muscles bunching and flexing as he moved. Her empath was quiet and smooth yet fought with a grace like no other.

Ellie killed two more wolves and turned to help Maddox with Corbin—who was stronger than them both—then screamed as another guard in human form pulled at her arm and flexed his wrists, breaking the bone in a sharp sting that flooded her body with pain.

Maddox turned at her scream then shouted.

Corbin smiled and pulled the knife out of her mate's side, Maddox's blood leaving a crimson stain on the blade.

The mating bond tightened in pain then pulsated, sending a scorching heat toward each of them as tears slid down her cheeks.

Goddess, it wouldn't end like this.

Out of the corner of her eye, she saw Charlotte pulling at her chains, working hard to try to break free.

At least the little girl was safe for now, but, goddess, Ellie needed to fight harder.

Despite the pain in her arm, she fought, clawing and tearing at what she could. Only three wolves remained, but she'd kill them all. She had to. Maddox continued to fight Corbin, even with the blood running down his side.

Finally, finally, she broke the last wolf's neck and

turned toward her mate. There had to be a way to end this. She took a step forward then screamed her body freezing.

Caym stood behind her, chanting a spell she didn't understand, but she could *feel* the bond between her and Maddox shaking.

"It's a lost cause, my dear," Caym drawled. "I have a perfect spell for you, and believe me, you'll break under the onslaught. Your Omega can't tamp down the emotions anymore. Now, everything he's ever felt is amplified, and since you're mated to him, you'll both feel *everything*."

The emotions suddenly flooding through her system, her mind, her nerve endings, rendered her speechless. Goddess, she could feel it all. The pain, the happiness, the sheer amount of the endless bonds, to not only the Redwoods but to something far darker. Her old bond to the Centrals that had been broken flared again, and she could feel the evil seeping through it and enveloping them. She and Maddox locked gazes and fell to the ground, their bodies shaking. She reached for Maddox as tears stained her cheeks.

Oh, goddess.

The pain.

They tried to fight the evil threatening to take hold but neither could breathe.

Everything seemed heavy, the weight on her chest capable of killing her.

Caym and Corbin laughed as they moved toward her.

Her brother picked her up, each point of contact between them a searing pain.

The darkness dripped off him, covering her like a thick blanket of hate and fear. They stepped over Maddox on the ground as he struggled to get up. Caym kicked him but didn't look down. Corbin chained her to the wall and smiled.

She hung from the wall, her toes barely touching the ground, her broken arm going numb, the pain so intense she nearly passed out.

Corbin took a step back and tilted his head. "I'm sorry that it had to end this way, dear sister. You should have been by my side all this time, but you ran away."

Everything around her seemed to pull her down, each movement became slow, heavy. She pulled her head up and looked into his black eyes.

"I'll never regret it," she said, her words slurred.

Corbin shook his head. "You won't have long to regret it."

Caym handed him something, but she couldn't tell what it was. Her vision had blurred from the pain and the influx of Pack bonds.

He raised his arm, and the light bounced off the barrel of the gun.

"Good bye, dear sister," he said and fired.

Her chest exploded, fire scorching her as she gasped for breath.

Her head fell forward, and she looked down, not really

understanding what had happened. With one last effort, she looked up at her mate, her Maddox.

He crawled toward her, bleeding, screaming.

Their bond screamed as well.

Ellie closed her eyes, her lids heavy.

The darkness took over.

22

Maddox screamed.

His throat burned as he yelled, his voice hoarse.

The mating bond throbbed then thudded to a quiet breath.

Oh, goddess, no.

Ellie's head lolled to the side as she hung from the wall, the large hole in her chest a stark reminder that everything had gone wrong, that everything had changed.

Though their mating bond had dimmed, it wasn't completely gone. It couldn't be. He tried to reach it and tried to pull her to him, at least through the bond, but he couldn't grasp it.

No.

Goddess, no.

The assault of whatever spell Caym had forced on him

still echoed through him, coming and going in shifts until it reared up again, knocking him back down to his stomach. There was no way he'd just stay there though. He'd get up and get his mate.

She was not dead.

There was no fucking way she could be dead.

He heard a whimper behind him, and he closed his eyes.

Charlotte.

Hell, he'd get her out too.

Ellie would be okay.

She had to be.

The salt from his tears tasted bitter on his tongue, and he forced himself to work through the pain in his side and in his bones. He lifted himself up and almost fell back down but forced himself to his feet.

Corbin and Caym were staring at Ellie, ignoring him.

Their mistake.

On shaky legs, Maddox rose and staggered toward his Ellie, his mate. Quietly, he lifted the knife that had been used on him from the table and moved.

Corbin turned in that moment, surprise on his face.

The knife slid into Corbin's heart like butter, the blade smooth, heavy in Maddox's palm as he twisted.

Corbin fell to the ground, his black eyes still wide in surprise. Caym turned on his heel and frowned. Without another word, Caym's arm shot out and slammed into Maddox's chest. Maddox hit the wall, sliding down to the ground, his chest on fire from his ribs most likely being broken.

Maddox watched under heavy lids as Caym cupped Corbin's cheek. It would have been an almost intimate gesture if there had been any emotion whatsoever on the demon's face.

Caym whispered something Maddox couldn't hear, and Corbin screamed. The bastard wolf's chest shook as Caym slide the knife out, leaving no wound behind.

Fuck.

It seemed it wouldn't be him who killed Corbin today. He only hoped what Corbin had thought was true, and North would be the one to do it and do it soon.

Caym picked up Corbin and made his way to the door, his process slow, labored. Apparently, the magic he'd used —twice in a row—had taken its toll on the demon.

Good.

Caym stopped at the door, having walked over the bodies Ellie had taken care of before.

"I'll give you ten minutes because I admire the way you surprised me, Omega. Ten minutes."

With that, the demon walked out the door, limping slightly.

Maddox pulled himself up, ignoring the searing pain and heavy magic pushing him down. He limped to Ellie first.

Goddess, no.

She had to be okay.

He slowly unhooked her from the wall. Corbin had been so sure of himself he hadn't bothered to lock the chains. After all, considering the curse Caym had thrown at them, what use was a mere lock?

His wolf howled as Maddox slid to the ground, Ellie in his arms. Her eyes were closed, and she looked completely white. He grit his teeth as another wave of emotion slammed into him, but not from his Ellie, and he brushed a lock of hair from her face.

The bullet had pierced her heart.

Her heart that was no longer beating.

Their mating bond slowly faded to almost nothing, but unlike the way Adam had lost Anna in that split second of severing, Maddox could still feel his mate, just not her life.

Another hit of whatever spell Caym had placed on him caused his body to convulse.

Hell, he was dying too.

His chest shook as he screamed again, his body convulsing in gut-wrenching sobs. He'd only just found her. He'd only just let himself believe he could be with her.

And now she was gone.

"I'm sorry," a little voice said from the corner, causing Maddox to look up with a growl.

Charlotte cowered in the corner, her collar now off her neck. The chain must have been pulled off the wall during the fight. Somehow the little girl looked okay, despite all that had happened around him. Yet she hadn't run away, instead staying with him and Ellie.

"It wasn't your fault," he said honestly.

Though they'd come to the den to save her, it wasn't her fault Maddox hadn't been strong enough to save his mate. It wasn't her fault that Corbin was a sadistic bastard and had killed his own sister.

Killed.

"Can you help her?" she asked, yet there was no hope in her voice.

He ran his hand through Ellie's soft hair, willing her to be okay, to come back to him. He looked up at Charlotte and started to shake his head then stopped.

There was still that bond.

Why?

Maybe his and Ellie's bond was stronger than most.

He also had all this extra energy and emotion running through him. Emotions were part of life, a life force unto their own. Maybe he could use what Caym had given him and save his mate. Hannah could heal even the worse of wounds, maybe he could use part of her power through the Pack bonds and whatever else he could.

Goddess he hoped so.

Caym had given him only ten minutes, and two had already passed. He closed his eyes and concentrated on the bond. It was there, thin and thready, but goddess, it was there.

He focused on that thread and found the other emotions running through him. He then funneled all he could through him and into that thread.

Sweat beaded on his forehead, and his body shook. He gasped as he felt a little hand on his forehead. He opened his eyes and stared into Charlotte's dark ones.

She looked like a miniature Ellie.

Tears slid down her cheeks just like his, and he closed his eyes again, leaning into Charlotte as he tried to breathe life into his mate.

The bond thickened, his wolf howling along with the energy flowing through them.

He opened his eyes again and looked down, willing his Ellie to come back to him.

"Ellie mine, come back. Please, I need you. I love you so much, Ellie mine. Come back."

Nothing happened, and his chest ached. He couldn't lose hope.

She had to come back.

He cupped her cheek and lowered his lips to hers.

"Ellie mine," he whispered.

Ellie gasped against his lips, her body stiffening in his hold. He watched as the wound on her chest knitted together, the energy that had been attacking him before now flowing through their bond, breathing new life within it.

"*Maddox.*"

He started. She hadn't said that aloud. That had been *inside* his head.

"*Ellie?*" he asked, using that same fragile path she'd used in their minds.

"What happened? And how am I hearing you in my head?"

He kissed her hard then pulled back. "We'll talk about it later, Ellie mine. Oh, God, you're back."

He kissed her again then felt another little hand on his shoulder. He looked up at Charlotte and nodded.

"We need to go, Ellie. Can you walk?"

Her arm and chest looked healed, but considering she'd just died, he had no idea how she would feel. They'd talk about it all and what this new power of theirs meant when there were safe. Now, though, they needed to go and find the Redwoods.

They needed their home.

Ellie nodded, and he staggered to his feet then pulled her up. Though his side still hurt like hell from where Corbin had stabbed him, the earlier pain from the attack of energy and emotions was now gone.

Whatever he had done to the bond by using that curse had helped not only Ellie, but himself as well.

He hugged her close again then lifted Charlotte into his arms, tucking her at his hip.

"Let's go."

"Why aren't Corbin and Caym here?" Ellie asked, her brow wrinkled.

"Caym gave us ten minutes to say goodbye, and we have about half of that. We need to go."

She nodded and walked by his side. Charlotte buried her face in his neck, and he took a deep breath. He'd deal with everything that had happened later. Right now, he needed to get his family out of this hell.

Caym and Corbin were nowhere to be seen, but he could feel other wolves circling them. He didn't know if the other wolves would agree to what Caym had said, or if they even knew the promise had been made. Maddox shook his head. It wasn't as if he believed the word of a demon anyway.

He ran as fast as he could to the weakest point on the wards, Charlotte in his arms and Ellie by his side. They'd done what they'd come to do—save Charlotte. He just hoped the consequences of that action, the unknown in what they'd done, didn't come back for them.

"Hurry, Maddox," Ellie said in his mind.

He nodded, still not used to this new connection of theirs, though the sound of his mate's voice made him want to weep with joy.

They made their way to the wards and stopped in front of the inky black magic. "Brace yourselves."

He took a step through, and Charlotte screamed in agony into his ear. He immediately pulled back, Ellie following him, and dropped to his knees to take a look at Charlotte.

"What is it? What hurts?" he asked, looking over her. He'd been so focused on Ellie he'd only given the little girl a cursory look.

God, what if he'd missed something?

She shook her head and placed her hand over her heart.

"I can't go through the wards. At least I don't think I can. Caym said he put a lock on me. Is that what he meant?"

It dawned on him then.

That vindictive bastard.

"Did he use a spell on you, baby?"

"I think so..."

Ellie reached out and pulled her sister into her arms—the first time the girls had touched. "I think it's because she still has those Central bonds, Maddox. I remember Corbin saying Caym was planning on forcing all the Centrals to stay within the wards unless on assignment. I hadn't known how he'd planned on doing that. Oh, God, Maddox. How are we going to leave?"

Maddox took a deep breath. "We're going to have to bring her into our Pack now." Fuck, this would hurt Charlotte like hell, and he prayed it could actually be done.

"Can we do that?" Ellie asked as she ran her hands up and down Charlotte's black.

Usually only the Alpha could bring a new member into a Pack if it wasn't a full mating, but they'd done it before with Willow, and later with Hannah and Josh, through partial matings and through forcing the bites.

They'd just have to chance it.

Hell, they didn't have another choice.

He looked around for a sharp object and cursed himself for not have brought the knife with him. Apparently, blood loss had officially made him an idiot.

He found a sharp stick and forced Charlotte to face him.

"I'm going to bring you into the Redwoods, Charlotte," he explained to the little girl with tears in her eyes. "It's gonna hurt, baby girl. We're going to have to sever the bond with the Centrals you were born with, and then we'll form a new one with my blood. In fact, to make sure it works, we're going to bond you with Ellie too. I don't know another way to make this work, baby girl. My dad could do it with just his wolf and magic, but we need the blood."

She nodded, her little face blank. "Okay. I want to go home with you. You guys are nicer than Corbin. I don't want him as a brother anymore."

He watched as Ellie bit her lip, trying not to cry, and he swallowed hard, trying not to cry himself.

"Okay then. Ready?" he asked.

She nodded, and he cut his palm then Ellie's. Since it was only a sharp stick, he had to press hard, and it hurt like hell. He then took both of Charlotte's palms and cut them. He and Ellie each took one of her hands, and he closed his eyes, letting his wolf do what he'd know to do.

The bond between him and Ellie pulsed then branched off toward Charlotte. He'd seen bonds form during the birth of his brother's children and knew that this was the child's bond, one that would fade away over time when the child grew up. His wolf was marking this child as his and, therefore, Pack It wasn't easy to bring in a Pack member, only the member of the Alpha's family could even attempt it.

Charlotte leaned into him and screamed in pain. Ellie murmured reassurances and leaned into Charlotte's other side. He held back his own anguish at hurting this little girl, knowing he had to be the strong one.

Finally, he could feel those sweet emotions threading through his Omega powers, and he knew Charlotte was now Pack.

Goddess, they could go through the wards now.

He looked up at Ellie and let out a breath.

"Let's get the hell out of here," he said, picked up the little girl, and gripped Ellie's had.

This time when they walked through the wards, though the pain was heavy and clawed at all of them, Charlotte didn't cry.

She wasn't a Central anymore.

She was a Redwood.

She was theirs.

They made their way to the end of the wards, and Maddox put Charlotte down. "We're going to have to move fast going back," he said. "We should run as wolves. I take it you can shift, right?"

Charlotte nodded then walked behind a bush, pulling off her clothes to shift without being asked.

He and Ellie did the same then shifted to wolves. A little brown wolf came out of the bushes and yipped at him.

He bit the scruff of her neck as Ellie licked her little muzzle, and then they were off. They ran toward the Redwoods as wolves, away from the Centrals that had taken so much of each of them.

They ran as the family he'd never expected to have—had never known he'd wanted.

Corbin and Caym would pay for what they'd done, and by the looks of their weaknesses in that room, they were already on that path.

It was only a matter of time and with any luck, he'd be there to see their end.

23

"*G*ood *morning, Ellie mine,*" Maddox said, smiling because he hadn't opened his mouth to do so.

"*Good morning, my wolf,*" Ellie said back, a smile in her own voice.

It had been almost two weeks since they'd come back from the Centrals, panting, their paws cut and bleeding, but alive. They were still just getting used to this new power of theirs, but they both loved it.

He could hear the thoughts she pushed to him as if she were talking, and she could do the same with him. They couldn't, however, hear random thoughts or anything from another person, nor could they hear each other's wolves.

Thank the goddess.

With his own thoughts, his own wolf, and now, Ellie, he had enough in his mind. He really didn't need another in there.

Of course, they also had their new bond—or rather their old one infused with whatever Caym had cursed him with—to learn to deal with. After he and Ellie had completed the mating with their marks, they'd shared the emotions that went along with his being an Omega. Now, it was as if this new way to bond had settled them both.

He could focus more now.

He could breathe again as he had before he'd become the Omega, when he'd been younger.

He no longer had that constant barrage of emotions that forced him to hide away in a corner and fear touching anyone in case it intensified their emotions. Unlike he'd feared for so long, Ellie wasn't in the fetal position rocking in pain as she dealt with all these new energies.

Everything was calmer.

He could now pick out individual emotions and help his Pack easier because he wasn't fighting it anymore. He was *living* it.

Whatever Caym had used to break open the blocks Maddox had put in place had actually *saved* him.

He'd never thank the demon, but goddess, he'd thank the woman currently in his arms for saving his life.

Saving his future.

Ellie wiggled in his arms, her soft bottom against his cock. They were lying in bed on a lazy morning, enjoying the fact that they didn't have to wake up until later as Charlotte was currently at his parents' house getting to know her new family.

His mother had fallen in love at first sight with the little girl, and now Charlotte would never again know what it meant to not feel love.

Ellie moved her hips again, and Maddox gripped her hip to take some control back.

"What are you doing, mate of mine?" he asked as he lifted his hand to move her hair back from her neck. He bent his head to lick and nibble the mate mark he'd put back on her the night before. It had been the fourth time he'd marked her and loved it each time. Each mark would fade over time as it healed, but the sensitive spot and what the mark stood for would never fade.

Because it *did* heal though, it gave mates an excuse to keep marking each other and reaping the rewards—they would get to come over and over again while they sank their teeth into each other throughout their lives together.

Ellie rolled her hips, forcing his cock to slide between her cheeks. "Just finding a way to wake you up."

Maddox gave a rough chuckle, moved his hand around her stomach, and circled her clit with his finger.

She shuddered in his hold, lifting her leg so he had better access.

Well, since she'd made it so easy...

He plunged his fingers into her wet pussy and ground the palm of his hand against her clit. She arched her back, and he kissed her mate mark again.

"Maddox, I don't want to come without you in me. Please, I want to feel you."

"If that's what you want, Ellie. You know I'd let you come over and over just to see the way that pretty skin of yours blushes." Even as he said it, he moved and pulled her leg to wrap around his then thrust into her.

Hard.

They both sighed at the same time, his dick hard and balls deep within her soft channel. He rubbed her clit again with each thrust, loving the way her pussy clenched around him as she rose toward her peak.

She moved her head so he could capture her lips, and he was lost.

"Goddess, I love you," he said, panting.

"I love you so much, Maddox."

As she spoke, he plunged hard, and she twisted her head to watch him. She came apart in his arms, her eyes widening and her mouth parting on a sigh.

He came with her, his seed filling her. He wanted it to take root so he could watch her grow round with his child. Then Charlotte would have someone to grow up with.

Ellie turned in his arms, and he smiled. "You're mine," he whispered.

"As you're mine. I love when you smile, Maddox. You're doing it more often."

He tucked a lock of hair behind her ear and kissed the tip of her nose. "I have more to smile about. I have a mate who loves me and stands by my side. I have a little girl who we get to watch grow up and love as much as we will our own children. Charlotte will grow up with two loving parents—even if she'll call us by our names. And I have my family, which is growing around me, and my Pack, which is growing stronger with each breath. I'm happy."

He was, he truly was. Before, he'd known things weren't perfect for him, but he hadn't realized how unhappy he'd been with his lot in life.

Now, he had Ellie and Charlotte.

Goddess, he was blessed.

After they got out of bed and got ready for the day— complete with a *very* steamy shower—they headed over to his parents' house. They were going to have a Jamenson dinner and talk about what their next plans were concerning the Centrals. Plus, Maddox wanted to see Charlotte and bring her home from her slumber party.

Who knew he'd love being a father?

Charlotte would probably always call him Maddox and Ellie by her name, but he knew that he'd always think of her as a daughter. Ellie had even told the little girl that she would raise her as a daughter and that they all three would learn together how to be a family.

After all, while Maddox had grown up with endless brothers and, eventually, a little sister, Ellie, like Charlotte, had never had a true family. She'd always had to be the strong one for her broken sister and cousin, the one who had to deal with the fact that her mother had been killed by her father, and the one who had to taken the brunt of Corbin's abuse.

Now, she had him and Charlotte, and he'd do all in his

power to make sure she knew she'd *always* have them.

They walked in the front door to hear Charlotte's giggle.

"Maddox," Ellie whispered, and he pulled her closer.

"I know," he said and kissed her neck.

While Charlotte was healing, they'd only heard her laugh or giggle a handful of times. He never thought he'd get enough of that precious sound.

Charlotte came running at them and threw herself into Maddox's arms. His heart filled as he filled his arms with little girl.

"Hey, lady-bug butt," he said as Cailin came running in behind.

"Hey, big brother, that was my nickname," Cailin teased.

Charlotte kissed his cheek, and he fell in love all over again. "I like it when you call me that. It means you like me like you like Aunt Cailin."

Yep, he was a pile of mush for this little one.

Ellie reached in and tickled Charlotte then gave each of them a kiss. "You look happy, darling."

Charlotte nodded. "Uh huh. Grandma Pat made cookies, and I got to help with the sprinkles. Parker did the cutting, but that's because he's older."

His mom had taken Charlotte in with open arms. Pat had wanted Charlotte to have grandma-time, hence why she'd spent the night. His mom had also fallen in love with Parker and was helping Lexi watch him when Lexi needed time to breathe.

It seemed their family was growing with each new day,

and Maddox, frankly, was damned happy about that.

Eventually, the younger kids were fed and put down for bed, and Parker had taken Charlotte, as well as Gina, to the playroom to play video games, leaving the adults at the dinner table, haggard and worse for wear, but alive.

The Centrals had beaten them at every corner, attacked them with each passing month, but the Redwoods were still breathing.

Kade and Melanie were not only raising Finn now, but also Larissa and Neil's children as their own—despite the problems that would arise with that since he was the eldest and Heir. They sat at their end of the table, leaning into each other. The sorrow that he'd seen in Melanie before he'd left was still there, but not as blatant. Larissa had been one of her only friends when she'd been a human, and, now, she was gone, but Melanie would one day be Alpha female and was stronger than she gave herself credit for.

Jasper and Willow sat across from them, they too leaning on each other. His brother looked more tired than usual, but with all that was going on within their Pack, it wasn't a surprise. His job as Beta was a demanding one, but Willow was there by his side.

Across from them, Hannah, Josh and Reed sat talking quietly, nibbling at their food. They'd been through so much but had come out stronger than ever. Maddox was just glad the unconventional triad was part of their family and on their side. After all, they were a force to be reckoned with.

Bay and Adam sat next to the triad, frowns on their faces as they discussed something in quiet tones. Maddox had never thought Adam would be truly happy after he'd lost Anna. Now, though his brother had lost his leg and almost his life to protect his family, he had a future.

North and Cailin sat near them, neither of them talking, while Lexi and Logan sat across from them, also silent. At first, Maddox had thought his father had invited Lexi and Logan to match make with North and Cailin since it was clear to everyone—except maybe the couples themselves—that there was something there, but then he thought maybe his father had another idea in mind.

"We're at war," Edward began, and all other conversations stopped. "We've gradually brought in new members to our Pack to strengthen our own." He took in those gathered around the table—Willow, Melanie, Josh, Hannah, Bay, Ellie, and then Lexi and Logan, who had been officially made Pack members the week before, along with Parker.

"We've been able to fight back against the Centrals, but we never strike first," his father continued. "We've never been able to have the upper hand because we don't use dark magic. We won't stoop down to their level and risk the world and our souls to win the easy way. In doing so, we've let the Centrals come to us, and that decision has made us weak."

Each of them growled but shut up when Edward raised a hand. "We've been weak because it's been forced on us... but no longer. We've trained our fighters and enforcers. Our next move is to take the fight to them. Maddox and Ellie have started this. They've hurt Caym and Corbin to their cores, and they are weaker for it. We now know Corbin is afraid of North. Something we can use."

Maddox held back a wince at that. He'd hidden that fact for so long to protect his brother and, in turn, had hidden a key to winning.

North nodded and ran a hand through his hair. "We can't tempt fate, nor can we stop its course, but I'll be ready."

Maddox watched Lexi's expression as North spoke. She looked like someone had struck her, yet she had hope in her eyes. He didn't understand it, but he didn't think it was for him to do so.

North and Cailin would accept their fates or fight them.

The Redwoods would win because they were stronger in their hearts than a demon with a motive that not one of them knew or understood.

Maddox wrapped his arm around Ellie's shoulders. He had his future now. He had his peace.

The Centrals couldn't take that away from him, no matter hard they tried—no matter how hard they *had* tried.

He kissed his mate's temple and sighed. He was the Omega, the one to soothe and fight for the emotions of the Pack, but it had been the love of one woman who had shown him what it truly meant to be at peace.

Ellie was his savior, his peace, and soon the Redwoods would find their own as a fighting force to be reckoned with.

EPILOGUE

Corbin winced as he looked in the mirror. Hell, he looked like shit. Damn fucking Omega had almost killed him. If it hadn't been for his lover, Caym, he'd have died.

Now, Caym looked weak, even if he said he would gain energy again. As if he'd used some of his own reserve to save him. Warmth slid through his cold, dark heart. Well, didn't that make him feel like he was loved?

Maddox had almost killed him and failed, but that didn't mean the seer had been wrong. North would be after him, and he had a feeling Maddox wouldn't be hiding the reason for his scar and lies for much longer.

He'd have to find a way to kill that twin soon.

He rubbed a hand over his chest.

He was also pretty sure he knew where *she* was, though she wouldn't be where she was for long.

It was damned time he found her.

Her and her brat.

The Redwoods had the one woman he couldn't keep, and they had his future.

He'd just have to make sure they didn't keep her.

Corbin smiled in the mirror.

He had just the way to ensure his plan.

****

Next in the series?

Its North's turn in Hidden Destiny!

You can see Maddox and Ellie in the special novella, Loving the Omega as well!

A NOTE FROM CARRIE ANN

Thank you so much for reading **SHATTERED EMOTIONS!**

Next in the series?

Its North's turn in Hidden Destiny!

You can see Maddox and Ellie in the special novella, Loving the Omega as well!

If you want to make sure you know what's coming next from me, you can sign up for my newsletter at www. CarrieAnnRyan.com; follow me on twitter at @CarrieAnn-Ryan, or like my Facebook page. I also have a Facebook Fan Club where we have trivia, chats, and other goodies. You guys are the reason I get to do what I do and I thank you.

Make sure you're signed up for my MAILING LIST so you can know when the next releases are available as well as find giveaways and FREE READS.

Happy Reading!

Redwood Pack Series:

Book 1: <u>An Alpha's Path</u>

Book 2: <u>A Taste for a Mate</u>

Book 3: <u>Trinity Bound</u>

Book 3.5: <u>A Night Away</u>

Book 4: <u>Enforcer's Redemption</u>

Book 4.5: <u>Blurred Expectations</u>

Book 4.7: <u>Forgiveness</u>

Book 5: <u>Shattered Emotions</u>

Book 6: <u>Hidden Destiny</u>

Book 6.5: <u>A Beta's Haven</u>

Book 7: <u>Fighting Fate</u>

Book 7.5: <u>Loving the Omega</u>

Book 7.7: <u>The Hunted Heart</u>

Book 8: <u>Wicked Wolf</u>

<u>The Complete Redwood Pack Box Set</u> (Contains Books 1-7.7)

Want to keep up to date with the next Carrie Ann Ryan Release? Receive Text Alerts easily!

Text CARRIE to 24587

ABOUT THE AUTHOR

Carrie Ann Ryan is the New York Times and USA Today bestselling author of contemporary, paranormal, and young adult romance. Her works include the Montgomery Ink, Redwood Pack, Fractured Connections, and Elements of Five series, which have sold over 3.0 million books worldwide. She started writing while in graduate school for her advanced degree in chemistry and hasn't stopped since.

Carrie Ann has written over seventy-five novels and novellas with more in the works. When she's not losing herself in her emotional and action-packed worlds, she's reading as much as she can while wrangling her clowder of cats who have more followers than she does.

www.CarrieAnnRyan.com

ALSO FROM CARRIE ANN RYAN

The Ravenwood Coven Series:

Book 1: Dawn Unearthed

Book 2: Dusk Unveiled

Book 3: Evernight Unleashed

Montgomery Ink:

Book 0.5: Ink Inspired

Book 0.6: Ink Reunited

Book 1: Delicate Ink

Book 1.5: Forever Ink

Book 2: Tempting Boundaries

Book 3: Harder than Words

Book 3.5: Finally Found You

Book 4: Written in Ink

Book 4.5: Hidden Ink

Book 5: Ink Enduring

Book 6: Ink Exposed

Book 6.5: Adoring Ink

Book 6.6: Love, Honor, & Ink

Book 7: Inked Expressions

Book 7.3: Dropout

Book 7.5: Executive Ink

Book 8: Inked Memories

Book 8.5: Inked Nights

Book 8.7: Second Chance Ink

Montgomery Ink: Colorado Springs

Book 1: Fallen Ink

Book 2: Restless Ink

Book 2.5: Ashes to Ink

Book 3: Jagged Ink

Book 3.5: Ink by Numbers

The Montgomery Ink: Boulder Series:

Book 1: Wrapped in Ink

Book 2: Sated in Ink

Book 3: Embraced in Ink

Book 4: Seduced in Ink

Book 4.5: Captured in Ink

The Gallagher Brothers Series:

Book 1: Love Restored

Book 2: Passion Restored

Book 3: Hope Restored

The Whiskey and Lies Series:

Book 1: Whiskey Secrets

Book 2: Whiskey Reveals

Book 3: Whiskey Undone

The Fractured Connections Series:

Book 1: Breaking Without You

Book 2: Shouldn't Have You

Book 3: Falling With You

Book 4: Taken With You

The Less Than Series:

Book 1: Breathless With Her

Book 2: Reckless With You

Book 3: Shameless With Him

The Promise Me Series:

Book 1: Forever Only Once

Book 2: From That Moment

Book 3: Far From Destined

Book 4: From Our First

Redwood Pack Series:

Book 1: An Alpha's Path

Book 2: A Taste for a Mate

Book 3: Trinity Bound

Book 3.5: A Night Away

Book 4: Enforcer's Redemption

Book 4.5: Blurred Expectations

Book 4.7: Forgiveness

Book 5: Shattered Emotions

Book 6: Hidden Destiny

Book 6.5: A Beta's Haven

Book 7: Fighting Fate

Book 7.5: Loving the Omega

Book 7.7: The Hunted Heart

Book 8: Wicked Wolf

The Talon Pack:

Book 1: Tattered Loyalties
Book 2: An Alpha's Choice
Book 3: Mated in Mist
Book 4: Wolf Betrayed
Book 5: Fractured Silence
Book 6: Destiny Disgraced
Book 7: Eternal Mourning
Book 8: Strength Enduring
Book 9: Forever Broken

The Elements of Five Series:
Book 1: From Breath and Ruin
Book 2: From Flame and Ash
Book 3: From Spirit and Binding
Book 4: From Shadow and Silence

The Branded Pack Series:
(Written with Alexandra Ivy)
Book 1: Stolen and Forgiven
Book 2: Abandoned and Unseen
Book 3: Buried and Shadowed

Dante's Circle Series:
Book 1: Dust of My Wings
Book 2: Her Warriors' Three Wishes
Book 3: An Unlucky Moon
Book 3.5: His Choice
Book 4: Tangled Innocence

Book 5: Fierce Enchantment

Book 6: An Immortal's Song

Book 7: Prowled Darkness

Book 8: Dante's Circle Reborn

Holiday, Montana Series:

Book 1: Charmed Spirits

Book 2: Santa's Executive

Book 3: Finding Abigail

Book 4: Her Lucky Love

Book 5: Dreams of Ivory

The Happy Ever After Series:

Flame and Ink

Ink Ever After